The Green God

SELECTED FICTION WORKS BY L. RON HUBBARD

FANTASY
The Case of the Friendly Corpse
Death's Deputy
Fear
The Ghoul
The Indigestible Triton
Slaves of Sleep & The Masters of Sleep
Typewriter in the Sky
The Ultimate Adventure

SCIENCE FICTION
Battlefield Earth
The Conquest of Space
The End Is Not Yet
Final Blackout
The Kilkenny Cats
The Kingslayer
The Mission Earth Dekalogy*
Ole Doc Methuselah
To the Stars

ADVENTURE
The Hell Job series

WESTERN
Buckskin Brigades
Empty Saddles
Guns of Mark Jardine
Hot Lead Payoff

A full list of L. Ron Hubbard's
novellas and short stories is provided at the back.

*Dekalogy—a group of ten volumes

L. RON HUBBARD

The
Green God

GALAXY
PRESS

Published by
Galaxy Press, LLC
7051 Hollywood Boulevard, Suite 200
Hollywood, CA 90028

Printed in the United States of America.

ISBN-10 1-59212-360-0
ISBN-13 978-1-59212-360-5

Library of Congress Control Number: 2007903548

Contents

FOREWORD   vii

THE GREEN GOD   1

FIVE MEX FOR A MILLION   27

STORY PREVIEW:
SPY KILLER   87

GLOSSARY   97

L. RON HUBBARD
IN THE GOLDEN AGE
OF PULP FICTION   105

THE STORIES FROM THE
GOLDEN AGE   117

Stories from Pulp Fiction's Golden Age

A ND it *was* a golden age.

The 1930s and 1940s were a vibrant, seminal time for a gigantic audience of eager readers, probably the largest per capita audience of readers in American history. The magazine racks were chock-full of publications with ragged trims, garish cover art, cheap brown pulp paper, low cover prices—and the most excitement you could hold in your hands.

"Pulp" magazines, named for their rough-cut, pulpwood paper, were a vehicle for more amazing tales than Scheherazade could have told in a million and one nights. Set apart from higher-class "slick" magazines, printed on fancy glossy paper with quality artwork and superior production values, the pulps were for the "rest of us," adventure story after adventure story for people who liked to *read*. Pulp fiction authors were no-holds-barred entertainers—real storytellers. They were more interested in a thrilling plot twist, a horrific villain or a white-knuckle adventure than they were in lavish prose or convoluted metaphors.

The sheer volume of tales released during this wondrous golden age remains unmatched in any other period of literary history—hundreds of thousands of published stories in over nine hundred different magazines. Some titles lasted only an issue or two; many magazines succumbed to paper shortages during World War II, while others endured for decades yet. Pulp fiction remains as a treasure trove of stories you can read, stories you can love, stories you can remember. The stories were driven by plot and character, with grand heroes, terrible villains, beautiful damsels (often in distress), diabolical plots, amazing places, breathless romances. The readers wanted to be taken beyond the mundane, to live adventures far removed from their ordinary lives—and the pulps rarely failed to deliver.

In that regard, pulp fiction stands in the tradition of all memorable literature. For as history has shown, good stories are much more than fancy prose. William Shakespeare, Charles Dickens, Jules Verne, Alexandre Dumas—many of the greatest literary figures wrote their fiction for the readers, not simply literary colleagues and academic admirers. And writers for pulp magazines were no exception. These publications reached an audience that dwarfed the circulations of today's short story magazines. Issues of the pulps were scooped up and read by over thirty million avid readers each month.

Because pulp fiction writers were often paid no more than a cent a word, they had to become prolific or starve. They also had to write aggressively. As Richard Kyle, publisher and editor of *Argosy*, the first and most long-lived of the pulps, so pointedly explained: "The pulp magazine writers, the best of them, worked for markets that did not write for critics or attempt to satisfy timid advertisers. Not having to answer to anyone other than their readers, they wrote about human beings on the edges of the unknown, in those new lands the future would explore. They wrote for what we would become, not for what we had already been."

Some of the more lasting names that graced the pulps include H. P. Lovecraft, Edgar Rice Burroughs, Robert E. Howard, Max Brand, Louis L'Amour, Elmore Leonard, Dashiell Hammett, Raymond Chandler, Erle Stanley Gardner, John D. MacDonald, Ray Bradbury, Isaac Asimov, Robert Heinlein—and, of course, L. Ron Hubbard.

In a word, he was among the most prolific and popular writers of the era. He was also the most enduring—hence this series—and certainly among the most legendary. It all began only months after he first tried his hand at fiction, with L. Ron Hubbard tales appearing in *Thrilling Adventures, Argosy, Five-Novels Monthly, Detective Fiction Weekly, Top-Notch, Texas Ranger, War Birds, Western Stories,* even *Romantic Range.* He could write on any subject, in any genre, from jungle explorers to deep-sea divers, from G-men and gangsters, cowboys and flying aces to mountain climbers, hard-boiled detectives and spies. But he really began to shine when he turned his talent to science fiction and fantasy of which he authored nearly fifty novels or novelettes to forever change the shape of those genres.

Following in the tradition of such famed authors as Herman Melville, Mark Twain, Jack London and Ernest Hemingway, Ron Hubbard actually lived adventures that his own characters would have admired—as an ethnologist among primitive tribes, as prospector and engineer in hostile climes, as a captain of vessels on four oceans. He even wrote a series of articles for *Argosy,* called "Hell Job," in which he lived and told of the most dangerous professions a man could put his hand to.

Finally, and just for good measure, he was also an accomplished photographer, artist, filmmaker, musician and educator. But he was first and foremost a *writer,* and that's the L. Ron Hubbard we come to know through the pages of this volume.

This library of Stories from the Golden Age presents the best of L. Ron Hubbard's fiction from the heyday of storytelling, the Golden Age of the pulp magazines. In these eighty volumes, readers are treated to a full banquet of 153 stories, a kaleidoscope of tales representing every imaginable genre: science fiction, fantasy, western, mystery, thriller, horror, even romance—action of all kinds and in all places.

Because the pulps themselves were printed on such inexpensive paper with high acid content, issues were not meant to endure. As the years go by, the original issues of every pulp from *Argosy* through *Zeppelin Stories* continue crumbling into brittle, brown dust. This library preserves the L. Ron Hubbard tales from that era, presented with a distinctive look that brings back the nostalgic flavor of those times.

L. Ron Hubbard's Stories from the Golden Age has something for every taste, every reader. These tales will return you to a time when fiction was good clean entertainment and the most fun a kid could have on a rainy afternoon or the best thing an adult could enjoy after a long day at work.

Pick up a volume, and remember what reading is supposed to be all about. Remember curling up with a *great story*.

—Kevin J. Anderson

KEVIN J. ANDERSON *is the author of more than ninety critically acclaimed works of speculative fiction, including* The Saga of Seven Suns, *the continuation of the Dune Chronicles with Brian Herbert, and his* New York Times *bestselling novelization of L. Ron Hubbard's* Ai! Pedrito!

The Green God

The Green God

S WIFTLY Lieutenant Bill Mahone of Naval Intelligence
pulled his automatic from its shoulder holster and crawled
along the side of the coffin, screening himself from possible
guards.

Against the dark sky he could see the outline of the mound
which marked the tomb of General Tao Lo, and around it
the many unburied coffins which might or might not house
the dead of Tientsin.

It was a dangerous mission that had brought Mahone
venturing into the night. He had convinced his commander
that they would not be able to stop the constant looting and
murdering that had cast a reign of terror over the city until
the Green God was back in its temple.

Tientsin's Native Quarter was half in flames; the dead were
heaped in the gutters. The Chinese were convinced that their
city would fall, now that their idol was gone. Before long
these fanatics might sweep into the International Settlement
and wipe it out.

Mahone had received a slip of paper that one of the natives
in the Intelligence Department had brought in. It had been
found in the Native Quarter, and the Chinese ideographs had
read, "A jade calling card for General Tao Lo." The general

had been dead for a year, but Mahone was convinced that the Green God had been hidden in his tomb.

Now Mahone, disguised as a Chinese coolie, had come alone to try and get the Green God from the general's tomb and save the city before it was too late.

As he crawled along the side of the coffin a cry rang out directly above him and he felt the bite of a knife in his shoulder. With a spring he catapulted away and looked back. A dark figure leaped to follow him! Mahone's automatic spat fire and the shadow by the coffin screamed in agony. In front of him he could see other shadows rising up like ghosts. The faint light fell on the blades of many knives. Vicious snarls were hurled at Mahone as the guards swept down on him.

Knives flashed. The automatic spat again and again. There seemed no end to these fanatics. Bodies hurled their fighting lengths upon Mahone.

With his empty automatic he clubbed and beat about him. He could feel the impact of his steel crashing down upon skulls, arms, bodies. Chinese were sweeping over him in a stifling mass. Knives bit into his flesh like white-hot irons.

He felt men go down upon him, beside him, as he brought his gun butt down. But each time he struck, another screaming demon leaped to take the empty place. His arm was aching with exertion. He was bleeding from many wounds, but he fought on relentlessly.

Feet kicked him in the face, talonlike hands sought his throat, knives lanced in for his heart. His hand was sticky from the blood of crushed skulls.

*Knives flashed. The automatic spat again and again.
There seemed no end to these fanatics.*

By rolling over and over he managed to baffle the knives which flashed above him. Suddenly he brought up against a coffin. Then, protected on one side, he tried to gain his feet.

But each time he rose as high as his knees, a body would launch itself into him, pinning him again to the ground. He was partially protected by the inert Chinese he had either killed or knocked unconscious, and hope that he might be able to escape welled up within him.

His left hand fell upon the hilt of a knife and he snatched it up, lashing at the air before him. He felt that blade catch again and again, but each time, he pulled it from the flesh it had met and threshed out for new targets.

The knife blade was growing sticky and he felt a hot trickle of moisture running down inside his sleeve. The salty stench of blood was in his nostrils as he fought.

He was almost exhausted when the rush stopped momentarily. He sprang up and stood for an instant looking about him. Then the charge closed in again and the fiendish impact of bodies almost forced him to the ground once more.

With a leap he gained the top of a coffin lid and stood there a moment, thrusting down into the mass below him. They were closing in at his back. He felt a knife gash his thigh.

With the barrel of his pistol held tightly in his hand he beat down into the writhing shadows which struck up at him.

He sprang clear of the clutching hands and hit the ground running. A swelling roar of sheer rage met this tactic as the guards saw their quarry escaping. With one accord they plunged after him.

Running with all the speed he could wrest from his tired body, Mahone dashed around the corners of the grim boxes and skirted the mounds.

Suddenly a shot rang out ahead of him, to be followed by another. Mahone zigzagged and tried to change his course. Flame burst out at him again.

A bullet caught him in the shoulder, whirling him about. He lurched, stumbled, tried to catch himself. With the momentum of his speed carrying him forward, he plunged, almost horizontal, into the side of a coffin.

The yells grew dim in his ears and he felt himself slipping into the dread black of unconsciousness.

When he regained his senses he felt himself held tight between two wooden walls which crushed at him. He tried to move his arms but he found that they were bound to his sides. His legs were lashed out straight and he could not bend his knees. Not a foot above his face, he could feel the presence of wood.

Suddenly he realized where he was. He was bound tightly in a coffin. The heavy lid had been placed above him. He was sealed in. And the smell of rotting flesh was making his senses reel.

He was helpless in the hands of the men who had stolen the Green God, turning Tientsin into a bedlam of murder. Did they think he was dead? Would they leave him there beneath that heavy lid to die?

Although the lid was not nailed down, as Chinese coffin lids never are, its weight was sufficient to resist any effort to move it from the inside, even if his hands were free.

7

Straining his arms into his sides and then out again, he found that he was powerless to release the strong ropes which held him.

He stared up into blackness, a panicky sense of failure taking hold of him. He had failed in his mission to return the Green God to its proper place in the temple, and in that failure he was about to die horribly.

The fetid air closed in upon him and seemed to weigh down and pin him in his gruesome confines.

Then, through the thick walls of his prison, he could hear the murmur of voices. He pressed his ear to the wood to hear better.

The soft cultured accents of a Chinese gentleman came to him. "If this foreign devil knew where to find the Green God, others will also come. We will take it to the House of So-Liang and hold it there for the master when he comes for it. You will stay here, hiding in a coffin, and when the messengers come, tell them to go to the House of So-Liang."

Mahone's heart raced as he heard those words. They thought he was dead, and they were about to remove the Green God to a well-known lair of thieves in the outskirts of Tientsin. Then he had been right about the whereabouts of the Green God. If he could only get loose!

But his heart plunged sickeningly as he heard the next words. "You will bury this foreign devil so that his fate will forever remain a secret."

They were going to bury him alive! He knew what that meant. Slow suffocation, going mad trying to breathe the poisoned air, buried alive and upright as the Chinese dead are buried. Suffocation standing upright!

The cultured voice came yet again. "He is bound securely and the devils within him will be thwarted in their attempts to escape. Thus we will be pursued by no demons. Have the men dig the grave."

Mahone heard the clank of a crude pick striking rocks and the scrape of a shovel picking up the dirt. He was lying there powerless, listening to the rattle of tools as they dug out his own grave.

They were digging a hole four feet square and eight feet deep. They would lift his coffin up and carry it to the opening. They would tilt it down and slide it upright into the hole. Then he would hear the rattle of stones and dirt coming in on top of him. And he would be sealed in forever, buried alive!

The thought gave him terrible strength and he threshed about in an effort to free an arm. Although freedom from this coffin would only mean a ready death at the hands of the fiends who were about to bury him alive, it was better to die fighting than passively. He struggled furiously.

After what seemed ages, he felt his coffin lifted up and felt it lurch as men carried it along. The silence was broken only by the soft footfalls of the bearers as they carried the box to the open grave.

But as they picked him up, another surge of strength had caused him to lift his arm upward with a jerk. The violence of the move made the bonds bite deep into Mahone's flesh, but hope flamed within him. For he had felt something give.

Only a fraction of an inch, but it meant that one of the knots was faulty.

Working feverishly, afraid lest his movements betray him to his pallbearers, Mahone repeatedly threw his arm toward the lid. And each time he felt it go just a little farther.

They were setting him down again and he knew that they were beside his grave. Mahone gritted his teeth against the rope burns on his bare wrist and threw up the arm again. This time there was only a slight resistance. Straining it up he felt the bonds give, come loose. His arm was free!

But then he realized the futility of the movement. The Chinese were all about him and before he could raise that lid, providing he could lift it from the inside, they would strike down upon him and there would be no question as to his mortality.

Nevertheless, he reached across his body and fumbled for the knot which held the ropes about his other arm. Pain shot through his hand as the savageness of his efforts tore a nail from his fingers.

They were lifting the head of the coffin now in preparation to sliding it into its upright position in the ground. Mahone paused in his attack on the second knot and tried to push up on the lid with his loose arm. But the weight was too great and the wood did not give the slightest distance.

Mahone felt the box coming upright and knew that strong arms were holding the lid in place. He sagged down slightly and his feet touched the bottom of the coffin. He tore again at the other knot.

His coffin was being held vertical. There was a moment

of inaction. Then Mahone found himself plunging down through space. The coffin hit with a heavy thud which jolted the timbers. Mahone's knees buckled under him as he hit and banged against the lid.

His hand had been jarred loose from its work on the knot, but now he returned it feverishly to the task. He knew not what he could do, but he knew that if he ceased to move, the terrible silence of that grave would close in upon and hold him helpless from sheer terror.

Above him he heard a shovel scrape and a quantity of loose dirt struck against the top of the box, rattled down along its sides. Another shovelful followed. And once again Mahone heard that awful sound of the gravel and sand striking against his gruesome prison.

Then his other arm came free. Thoughts of escape flashed through his mind. Then he gave an inaudible gasp of relief as he hit upon a possible plan.

He threw his weight against the vertical lid. With a slight creak it fell a short distance back from the top of the box. Mahone put his two arms above him, plugging the opening the lid had left.

Gravel rattled down swiftly. It brought the dust in upon him and he choked from the suffocation of it. He felt sharp stones hit against his forearms as he held them up. The weight of the dirt coming from above was painful.

Then the rattling stopped and Mahone knew that he was imbedded in the grave and that the Chinese above him were filling in what remained of the hole. Soon there would be just a mound up there to mark his grave.

Mahone knew that he was rapidly exhausting the oxygen in the small space and that he must work quickly before the stale air rendered his strength useless.

He withdrew his forearms and felt dust and stones crash down over his body into the coffin. He stepped upon the pile they made and clawed at the loose dirt above him with frantic fingers.

Little by little the dirt came down and crept up on the floor of the coffin. And as it crept up, Mahone stood upon it and brought more down. He was rapidly opening a hole outside the coffin and he prayed that he would be able to reach the top before the fetid atmosphere robbed him of his strength.

Then he was able to project his body partway through the hole left by the sagging cover and he quickly opened enough space on top of the coffin to allow him to leave the interior behind him.

The dust which hung thickly in the darkness was in his throat and the dirt itself was through his hair and clothes. Finally he found that he could crouch on top of his former prison and he clawed up and up until he could finally stand. A good-sized chunk of dirt came down with his fingers and cool air suddenly swirled in about him.

He was free! With his arms laid out along the surface, he pulled himself up partway and then he stopped to listen. He realized that even though the others might be gone, there would still be a guard here to inform messengers as to the whereabouts of the Green God.

But the night lay still and heavy among the graves and he

pulled his long body all the way up to stretch thankfully on the ground to rest.

As he lay there a low voice fell upon him. As nearly as he could guess, it was on the other side of the tomb of General Tao Lo.

With the one thought in mind that he must get to the House of So-Liang to recover the Green God, Mahone climbed to his feet and prepared to slip away.

A shrill cry split the night behind him to be followed by still another. Mahone took to his heels and ran rapidly among the mounds, trying to put distance between himself and his pursuers.

He could hear their calls less than a hundred feet behind him and he knew that even in this darkness a running man could easily be seen. But his strength was going fast and he knew that he would not hope to last very long at the present pace.

Putting every ounce of energy into one burst of speed, he raced across the dark plain. Ahead of him he could see a mound of fair size and he darted around it. The calls of his pursuers were perilously close, but he threw himself at full length on the ground and waited breathlessly. At his hand he could feel the side of a coffin and he hugged it closely, praying that he might not be discovered.

He heard the rapid patter of running feet coming closer to him. Several shrill cries came from the vicinity of the large mound.

He was certain that the rasping of his breath would cause

him to be discovered, for the baffled cries were coming close to his hiding place.

Pressing against the side of the grim box, Mahone prepared to leap at the throat of the first man who discovered him.

He had not long to wait, for a Chinese rounded a corner of the box and stood there staring down, too startled to cry out. Mahone sprang for his throat, closed viselike fingers about the man's windpipe. There was no outcry, only a choking sob.

Something flashed down out of the convulsing yellow hand and Mahone laid the body on its back and stooped to pick up the man's weapon. It was a long, sharp knife.

Gripping the hilt, Mahone crept on. The sounds of the searchers were growing faint as they worked their way from the mound.

Soon they would discover the absence of one of their number and Mahone slid rapidly along, trying to put enough distance between himself and the others before that time of discovery came.

Ahead of him flickering lights told him the position of the Native City, and still cautiously, lest he be followed, he made his way toward them.

Once in the outskirts he felt easier. Although he was bloody and dirty, he was still possessed of the yellow dye and his black hair. And filthy Chinese, gashed and bloodstained, were all too frequent in these days of rioting and murder.

Walking along the wall of a muck-filled street, he came upon a marketing square. Slipping through the excited crowds and stepping over an occasional corpse in a gutter, Mahone found himself in the street of the House of So-Liang.

Above him the sky glowed faintly red by the light of burning homes, and in his ears came the roar of a faraway mob running amuck.

He knew that the one chance of restoring a semblance of order to the Native City and of saving the International Settlement lay in replacing that strange Green God back in its temple. Chinese, convinced that the city would fall during its absence, were, themselves, bringing about the downfall of Tientsin.

A black opening in the wall loomed ahead and Mahone found that he was on the threshold of the House of So-Liang, which passed as an inn but which was, in reality, the hangout of the most vicious thieves in all this city of thieves and murderers. To enter might mean death, but not to enter meant the flaming ruin of the city. Mahone felt of the knife in his tattered coat and plunged into the darkness.

A streak of dirty light and a babble of voices met him as he turned a corner in the dark alley. A low doorway opened in the wall and Mahone stepped through.

A squalid scene met his eyes. Ragged, evil Chinese with darting eyes sat cross-legged along the walls or about a blanket in the middle of the floor.

About the blanket the men sat playing some gambling game with short pieces of colored bone. Some of them glanced up as Mahone entered and then looked back to their play. On the blanket Mahone could see rings and gold coins. The thieves were gambling away their loot.

15

Mahone took a seat with his back to the wall, pretending to drop his head in sleep. But in reality it was to hide the betraying gray of his eyes.

Watching covertly he waited for some sign.

A Chinese officer entered and spoke to two men at the gambling table who immediately picked up their stakes and left the play.

But Mahone had heard just enough. The voice had been the same as that at the graves!

The yellow trio walked back through the room and mounted the rickety stairs at a far corner. Mahone watched them pass up out of sight. He heard a door slam overhead and the sound of straw-slippered feet on the planks.

Waiting until he could rise unnoticed, he walked toward the stairs. He had reached the first step when he heard a door slam above him. It was too late to stop now and he went on up.

Steps came down to meet him but he dared not look up for fear the descending Chinese would notice the gray eyes. Mahone felt a hand snatch at his shoulder and he looked up with an involuntary jerk. It was the Chinese officer again.

The Chinese stared at him for a second before Mahone lowered his head. But that second was enough, for the officer had seen the betraying color. With an oath he leaped down for Mahone.

There was no stopping now or arguing. Mahone picked up the other as though he were a child and threw him down to the first floor. The Chinese screamed out an order, and, as one, the gamblers and men along the walls rose up to race toward the stairs.

16

Mahone whipped out the knife in his coat and braced himself to meet the rush. To race on up the stairs would be useless. He was trapped and he could only try to fight it out with these howling demons below.

The first reached him, a shimmering blade ready to swoop down upon Mahone. But the American's knife flashed and came back into position for a second strike. The first Chinese fell back impeding the progress of his mates.

Two men snatched at Mahone but the deadly knife flashed down twice. The two had barely time to fall back, clutching at their throats, before the horde swept upon him.

The flickering yellow light glittered from drawn blades. Chinese were swarming up over the railing, trying to get at his back. To evade these, Mahone gave ground slowly. His knife was a streak of metal which seemed everywhere at once.

He looked down into faces, bloodshot eyes and foam-flecked mouths which snarled. He withstood the lunges of the filthy bodies as they pressed him up and back.

His right hand clenching the repeatedly striking knife, he sent his left fist into the mass, felt his knuckles striking home.

A knife gashed his arm and he whirled to see that the Chinese were pouring over the railing, getting at his back.

Pressing himself to the wall and fighting now on three sides at once, he inched up, trying to get above the end of the railing. Once there he could turn and meet them only from the front.

In the mass below he saw an arm swing up and a flash of hurtling steel. He shrank back just in time to avoid the thrown blade. It quivered in the wooden wall beside his shoulder.

He was steadily creeping up. One last Chinese stood above him. He flashed down with his knife and missed. Hands tore at his throat. A knife gashed his leg from below.

Utilizing a precious second, Mahone reached out and seized the writhing body above him. Turning, he threw the Chinese straight into the faces of his assailants below.

Now he could hold out as long as his strength would last. He was fighting them away from him in front. Now and then he kicked out at a jaw with his foot and felt the crunch of bone under his toes.

His knife lanced down to meet a leering face which sprang at him. He felt the steel rasp into flesh and bone, but the Chinese jumped back and plunged down, Mahone's knife still in his face.

Weaponless now, Mahone resorted to his two fists. Hammering relentlessly at the mass which pressed up, he managed to keep those death-blades away from his vitals and those tearing hands away from his throat.

He knew that he could not last forever, for where he was one, there were many more at their call.

He became conscious of a bellowing voice shouting from the mass below. One by one the snarling faces drew away.

Suddenly he was left alone on the stairs and he stood there, his arms hanging wearily at his sides, staring down. Dully he wondered what had happened, but then he knew.

The Chinese officer was standing at the foot with drawn automatic. The last Chinese out of range, the officer prepared to fire.

Mahone stared down into the black muzzle for a fraction

of a second, then he turned to leap up the stairs. He expected to hear that fatal shot at point-blank range any instant.

But he had almost reached the top before the pistol barked. Untouched, Mahone leaped up to the top and gazed wildly up and down the hall.

That second's hesitation cost him dear. For above him he glimpsed an upraised club which was descending with terrible speed. He raised his arms, trying to ward off the blow, but he was too late.

For the second time that night he was unconscious in the power of these maniacs who had plunged Tientsin close to the brink of destruction.

When he awoke he tried to rise, feeling himself forced down to the floor once more. He was weak from loss of blood and the fight on the stairs.

Dazedly he looked up and found that he was in a large room which was ornate in its decoration. He reasoned that he was on the second floor of the House of So-Liang, for they would scarcely bother to carry him any further.

Silk draperies were folded against the walls and the single lamp in the middle of the room shimmered from the dull colors of the light material. Seated in a chair at a table beside him was the Chinese officer. Kneeling at his head were two guards, prepared to hold him down.

He saw the light glance dully from their stained teeth, and the odor of their filthy bodies was strong about him. Once more he tried to move, but the Chinese officer at the table pointed an automatic at his stomach.

"Foreign devil," leered the officer, "I do not know how you

found our hiding place, but I do know that you will live to regret it, even though you do not live long. While we wait we will amuse ourselves with you."

Mahone closed his lips tightly but said nothing. He was a prisoner again, and he probably faced a more awful death than he had in the grave. While he was yet alive there was hope, though he wondered if it would not be better to let that automatic belch death at him.

"You wanted to know the whereabouts of the Green God." The Chinese officer's voice was smooth and deadly. "Many men would like to know this. You have seen the Green God? No? Well, look at it before you die."

A third guard who stood against the light silk hangings was ordered to fetch something from across the room. It was a silk-wrapped parcel.

The Chinese officer pulled back the wrappings and Mahone found himself staring up at a blaze of green light.

The Green God was jade, probably twenty pounds of the finest jade. But that was not the key to its value. For about its neck, hanging down over the fat green chest, was a string of large pearls which glowed in the light. And the eyes glittered from the red fire of two huge rubies. On the fat folded hands there were immense diamonds.

In spite of his peril, Mahone gasped at this show of brilliance. Never before had he seen anything to equal it. No wonder the Green God had been the source of so much murder and rioting!

He had only to reach up and take the thing, return to the

headquarters of Naval Intelligence and peace would reign once more over Tientsin. But the barrier there was as invisible as it was awful. Death by torture!

The Chinese officer replaced the wrappings. "Now that you have seen it, it is a pity that you will be unable to tell about it." He gave the third guard an order and the Chinese left the room.

Mahone waited tensely for his return. He dared not think of the fate which awaited him, for Chinese torture is known for its exquisite cruelty. He lurched up once more but strong arms held him tightly. He resorted to the better course of allowing his strength to return to his racked body. Perhaps there was some way out of this. And again, perhaps not. Even if he got out of the room he would never be able to reach the street alive!

A door slammed in back of his head and the guard approached the officer, two items in his hands. Mahone saw that they were a rattrap full of terrified rodents and an old earthenware pot.

Shudderingly he wondered what manner of torture could be devised with these two objects, but he was not long in finding out.

The Chinese officer stepped to his side and drew back the coolie coat, exposing Mahone's white abdomen. The American tried to roll sideways, but the guards held him still.

The third guard went out again and returned with two men. These took their places at Mahone's legs. He kicked at them but they gripped him and held on tightly.

The officer then took the cage of rats and, carefully blocking the edges of the vessel, held up one end. He placed the door of the rat cage inside the pot and the third guard poked at the animals, making them enter the vessel.

Mahone's flesh began to creep as he felt those sharp claws racing over his abdomen. Something like terror was beginning to crawl over him. He watched the officer lash the vessel tightly to his stomach.

It was not until then that Mahone knew what was about to happen to him. For the Chinese picked up an unlit pitch torch from the floor and carefully applied a slow-burning match to the head.

Mahone knew that they would press that torch to the top of the pot. He knew that the vessel would become untouchably hot. And that the heat would throw the enclosed rats into a panic. The rats had only one method of escape. They could not claw and tear their way through the heavy pot, but they had something soft and resisting below them. They would tear away from that heat and rip into Mahone's stomach. They would lay bare his skin and burrow deep into his intestines!

The awful realization of the hideous death he was about to meet gave Mahone new strength and he twisted about, attempting to dislodge the pot. But the leering Chinese about him pressed him back with a force born of cruelty.

The torch was flaring up now, sending new shadows leaping about the room. The Chinese officer came slowly to Mahone's side and touched the top of the earthenware pot with the flame. He held it there for a moment.

Close above his head was the silken curtain. Mahone fought down the terror inside of him and thought rapidly. He knew that silk was highly flammable. If there was only some way to get loose!

The claws were plunging deep. In a second it would be too late. Agony gripped him, and the air blurred red with pain. He threshed out with his right arm and threw one of the guards slightly off balance. He twisted his wrist with a violent jerk. The rats were going deeper.

He felt his arm come free, felt coarse fingers attempting to regain it. Heaving up he snatched at the light silk. With a shimmering billow it suddenly tore loose from its hangings. Mahone brought his arm down, lashing the silk across the torch.

His action had been so rapid that the officer had had no time to reach for the automatic or withdraw the torch.

Flame shot up from the drape. With a cry the guards jerked back. Mahone reached up again and ripped down another drape, throwing it over the first.

Then he was free beneath a pyre of flame. His hands caught at the pot. It withheld his efforts for a moment and then came away. With a quick slap at his middle, Mahone knocked away the burrowing rats.

He leaped up, away from the flames which had almost engulfed him. He saw that the silken robe of the officer was on fire, that the guards were beating at the flame on their own clothes.

Mahone jerked down other draperies and wrapped them

around him tightly to stifle the tongues of fire which licked at his trousers. Then he jumped to the task of throwing everything flammable onto the roaring blaze he had started.

Two objects on the table caught his attention and he jumped through the red heat to snatch them up. One was the Green God, the other was the automatic pistol of the officer.

Unnoticed in the bedlam which had arisen, Mahone plunged through the door. He had yet to beat his way through the mass of thieves and murderers below. At the head of the stairs Mahone stared down.

The Chinese on the first floor had heard the screams of the officer and guards and they were surging up the stairway to meet him. Mahone plunged down to meet them halfway. He shot straight into the mass of yellow faces.

Still charging down, he shot again and again. But there was no cutting through that mass. The automatic clicked empty and Mahone stopped to let them reach up to him.

For a second time that night he was using the butt of a gun for a club. He felt himself hampered by the twenty-pound Green God under his arm and he shifted it about. Then he realized its value, for the wrappings had become undone and the idol was hanging by two feet of heavy silk. Mahone swung it about his head like a sling, felt it crash on faces and bodies before him.

Slowly they gave way before him until he was almost at the bottom of the stairs. Unnoticed by the yelling Chinese, smoke had begun to creep down the stairs to them. In a moment the whole structure would be a mass of flame.

He glimpsed a tongue of scarlet shoot down through the

ceiling to be followed by others. The floor would not hold out much longer, and he must get through!

A blazing roof beam crashed down on the mob. He fought, whirled around to stare up.

Now was his chance! With a mad lunge he threw himself among them. Above him he could see the upper floor starting to come down.

He was running a race with fire, for if that beam crashed before he could make the door, the fate of the Green God would forever remain a mystery, and death would be even worse than the torture he had just escaped.

The Chinese were still staring up, unable to comprehend what was taking place. Mahone was among them, halfway through to the door, when the far corners of the room plunged down. Then the entire mob began to race for the door.

But Mahone had the start on them and he saw the black opening loom up in front. Behind him he heard a terrific crash as the entire ceiling came down. A burning beam struck him a glancing blow on the shoulder. Dying screams beat upon him.

The night was cool outside as Mahone plunged on down the twisting alley. Now if he could carry this burden safely through the Native City, Tientsin would be restored to normalcy.

In the street the howling mob was racing by, intent on loot and murder. Mahone dashed in among them and screamed as loud as any. He was racing in the direction of the International Settlement. At a corner, Mahone left the crowd and ran on toward his goal. He bent his steps to the office of Naval Intelligence.

A wild, blood-spattered being crashed through the door of the NI office and lurched to a stop in front of the commander's desk.

The commander drew a pistol and backed away. Then he threw the gun down and came forward. "Mahone!"

Mahone sagged against the desk, suddenly aching with weariness. "Yes, Mahone," he answered. "I haven't got it in my hip pocket, but here's your Green God!" He dropped the silken parcel on the desk and drew back the wrappings.

Undamaged, the Green God sat there smiling contentedly.

"You'll have to get it to the temple, Commander," Mahone continued. "I'm done in."

"Mahone!" cried the commander, dazzled by the brilliance of the idol. "You've saved the city!"

But Lieutenant Bill Mahone, NI, slumped to the floor to stare up at the grinning god. "I hope he appreciates all I did for him tonight."

Five Mex for a Million

Chapter One

EVERY eye in the smoke-dimmed interior was hostile. The silence which followed my entrance was thick with meaning. Not one man there dared stand up and shake my hand. Not one man dared to call me his friend.

I knew what they were thinking. Killer! Outcast! Renegade! Wanted man!

But neither did they dare blast me down for blood money. I smiled a little when I saw that. I edged up toward the long bar and signed my order to the Chinese boy who stood like a statue, arrested in the act of polishing a Tom and Jerry glass.

Looking about the room I saw eyes shift to avoid mine. Several men had played poker with me, had introduced me to their friends with a proud flourish. "Captain Royal F. Sterling, meet . . ."

No, I saw that no welcome awaited me in Peking. They were sour. Their political bread was buttered by other knives than mine.

The Chinese shoved the whiskey at me as though I might bite his hand, and then hurriedly retreated toward his fellows at the other end of the bar as though in great need of company.

The North China wind was blasting at the low structure, whistling shrilly through the cracks in the well-built room, howling as it rounded the corner of the club. The night was black and filled with dust. Winter had come to Peking.

I fingered a coin in my pocket. It was all I had—five Mex and that coin. And I needed money—not a few dollars, but thousands. I'd have to buy my way out of this, past the guards of the borders, through the police, from the soldiers.

The drink warmed me and took the blue chill out of my heart. For days this terrible sensation had been with me, riding me. I was trapped in a country almost as large as the United States. I couldn't get out, I couldn't stay. Now, looking at these white men in the club, these models of their nations, I felt a restless urge to raise hell as long as I lasted—and I knew that it wouldn't be long.

An American with a set, round face rose cautiously from his chair. He had been sitting alone. From the cut of his gray coat I knew that he was well-to-do. His ears were large and pointed and his mouth was a dark line above a square chin. He came slowly over to me and eyes followed him. The silence in the room deepened. It seemed to me that I had met him somewhere. Yes, his name was Compton. Frederick Compton, representing a huge trading firm in the States.

When he came within three feet of me he stopped heavily. From his pocket he took a sheet of paper and threw it down in front of me. I looked around, making certain that nothing would happen if I took my eyes off the room.

The notice was mimeographed. A crude five thousand had been drawn across the top and below it followed half-printed letters:

Five thousand dollars, gold, will be paid to that person offering information leading to the arrest and conviction of Captain Royal F. Sterling late of the 20th Route Army, wanted by authorities for the murder of Liang-Tsi-Wu.

Captain Sterling is five feet eleven inches in height. Weighs one hundred and sixty-five pounds. Brown hair, light gray eyes.

When last seen was dressed in riding boots, whipcord breeches and leather trench coat.

It is thought that he is heading toward Peking. Report any knowledge of his whereabouts to General Hseng, commanding the armies of the North.

"Thanks," I said, giving the notice back.

"Thanks, hell!" roared Compton with unnecessary vigor. "You're a killer! What right have you got coming here, putting our necks in a noose? What right? You're not wanted here. Get out! Do you hear me? *Get out!*"

I went on with my drink, taking it as slowly as I could. Nothing was waiting for me outside but the noisy wind and, perhaps, a firing squad.

It would be useless to tell these men that I hadn't killed Wu. They didn't care about that. Besides, I had killed him—one half second before his gun would have killed me. But Wu was dear to the heart of the unseen powers that govern the destinies of China and it seems that they were not particularly pleased about it.

Compton's face puffed up and turned a dark red. He stepped closer to me. His hand reached out as swift as a striking snake and slammed the whiskey glass out of my hand, spilling its contents across the shining bar. A gasp went through the room.

Compton's hand dived inside his coat, but before the fingers could bring forth the glint of blue which lay half-hidden there, I produced a .45 automatic from the pocket of my trench coat and buried the front sight in his rubbery stomach.

"Compton," I said, as quietly as I could, "that was a very foolish sort of thing to do. If it's a habit, I'm afraid you won't live long."

"I'll outlive you," he said gutturally. "Right now they're poking through every refuse dump in the city trying to find you. We're doing you a favor to—"

"You're not doing me any favor, none of you." I looked around to include those twenty others spread through the blue room. Legation attachés, diplomats, men of position and wealth. "If any of you need five thousand dollars, why don't you stand up and make a fight for it? It's easy enough to get. Just plug me and lug the corpse over to regimental headquarters. You're not keeping clear because of any love for me. No, I was great guns while I lasted. I was your best asset. 'Sterling, can't you do me a little favor? General Hseng . . .' And I came here tonight, like a fool, thinking I could get money to make a run for it."

Silence fell again except for Compton's wheezing. I withdrew my gun and pocketed it. Then I held his coat open and pulled out his .38, laying it down in the puddle of whiskey on the bar.

I turned my back on them and walked to the door. Not a chair scraped behind me—and a lot of men could have used that five thousand. I was disgusted with myself for ever having thought them my friends. They were too yellow to shoot me.

A blast of wind and gray dust slashed at me as I opened the door. Paper rattled in the room behind me. I slammed the door solidly, blocking off the yellow square of light which had lain an instant on the paving stones.

It was as though I had slammed the door of my past and everything that had surrounded me. And all because an excitable Chinese had thought I needed killing and had never thought it necessary to practice his draw.

My hands went deep into my pockets. I bowed my head and waded into the gale. The crumpled five Mex and the silver coin seemed very small between my fingers. I hadn't paid for my drink and somehow the fact made me a little ashamed.

No place to go. But if I stumbled about the streets of Peking all night the guard would pick me up and that would be the end of it. I had to do something.

Morrison Street was a long, black void. A few lights were almost blotted by the whirling dust. I went east, hugging the buildings and the shadows. Several times I saw soldiers with fixed bayonets, heads shaggy in their fur caps, looking like great bears in their cotton-padded overcoats.

If I meant to escape detection I would have to get rid of these clothes. But where in all Peking could I procure a full shift for five Mex? I knew of no place. But wait, it was after midnight and even in this bitter cold one place and one alone would be open. And they'd never think to look for me there.

The Thieves' Market.

After midnight the long, low shed southeast of the Forbidden City would house the criminals of Peking. It was a strange custom, this lawful bartering of stolen wares, but then perhaps the officials of some long-gone dynasty had thought it would prevent the evil of the fence. No thief could be arrested at the market. He was free to dispose of what he had stolen. The buyer might take the goods away and as long as they remained unidentified they were his. For that reason prices were very low.

Yes, I could obtain a suit of clothes at the Thieves' Market for five Mex. I could pass as a Chinese merchant from the North, going to Tientsin to see his son. I decided upon my name and the exact nature of my trade. If I only had brown eyes! No Chinese of my acquaintance had ever had eyes of silver gray. But then a pair of dark spectacles would remedy that. Yes, it would be very sad. The bandits had tried to blind me and I was seeking the home of my son in Tientsin. Maybe I could even get to Taku and the ships. I knew that I would need money, but that would have to take care of itself.

Outside the warehouse-like shed a few carts were pulled up to the curb, lanterns bobbing as the wind buffeted them. The owners were seated stolidly on the pavement, waiting for customers who did not come. Candied crab apples on sticks, powdered tiger whiskers, cinnamon salve for boils, any one of a hundred different things were to be gotten at those carts.

The market was queerly silent. A few men stood about, collars upturned and shivering. They paid no attention to me as I passed. The thieves were here but the night was too cold and wild for many customers. That was good for my purpose. They would sell me anything for next to nothing. When morning came, their wares would be liable to confiscation by the real owners, but not tonight.

The gray dust of Peking sifted through everything, more terrible because of the bitter coldness of it.

The place was like a tomb. Stolen goods had been dumped here and there upon the not-too-clean floor. The thieves or their agents crouched beside their wares, too cold to drum up business.

I saw a pile from which several garments sprawled. The thief was a small, withered person in a dirty gray cotton long coat, crouched with his hands in his sleeves, head down. I shook his shoulder vigorously. His eyes were dark and filled with misery. When he understood that a buyer had really come, he got up stiffly and began to talk of his wares in a weary voice.

He had evidently robbed a clothing shop of the better class. His goods were all new and bright. But as he held the lantern high above them to show me their quality, the slanting yellow rays fell upon an ancient piece of brass behind him.

He had been using a large chest for a backrest. An ancient blackwood box, it was fully six feet in length, edges bound in dull brass. It had three locks, but what interested me most was the design which had been carved on the top. Three dogs with nine tails apiece were there—one dog for each character.

The characters were: "Good luck! Long life! Happiness!" Common enough I admit, but I was miserable and cold and the thought of good luck and long life and happiness was reviving.

When he understood that a buyer had really come,
he got up stiffly and began to talk of his wares in a weary voice.

I pointed at the chest, suddenly interested, "What is in that?"

He looked long at me and then shrugged. "The contents must remain secret. I myself do not know the contents. Men brought it to me tonight and told me to sell it, but they gave me no keys. The buyer must purchase upon the condition that he does so without opening the chest. You like?"

Curiosity was eating at me. The three characters promised so much. And I needed a talisman. I hefted one end and found it very, very heavy. I gazed at the strong locks and decided that nothing short of a maul would break them.

Then, surprised at my own foolishness, I turned to the thief and watched him sort out more clothes. But I couldn't keep my mind upon it. Good luck, long life and happiness. And the contents were unknown and a buyer couldn't open it to see what he was buying.

Practically staring into the muzzles of a firing squad, I still found time to wonder about a chest which surely couldn't concern me in any way. Curiosity, I told myself. Get your clothes and beat it. But the hunch stayed with me.

"Let me see what is within," I said.

He shook his head. "How much you pay?"

The thought of buying it had not yet come to me, then the hunch swelled into a sizzling flame and I knew I'd spend the rest of my life—however long or short—wondering what could be inside the thing.

"Very good chest. Maybe gold inside. Worth much, much money, I sell very cheap. Very dear. Worth much, much money."

He hadn't displayed any eagerness in trying to sell the clothes, but he wanted to get rid of the chest. I saw that the thing had been worrying him and that he wanted to be shut of it as soon as possible.

"One Mex," I said.

He grunted and went back to the clothes.

"Two Mex," I said.

He paid no attention.

"Three Mex," I offered. And in the back of my head buzzed a voice which told me I was being a colossal fool.

He straightened up. His face was impassive by the uncertain light of his wind-hammered lantern. "Five Mex, you take. I want no more. I want no less. Five Mex, you take."

Almost before I could stop myself I had the five-Mex bill out of my pocket. Outside of that silver coin, it was all I had. No clothes, no escape. "What the hell," I said in English, and shoved the grimy bill into his hand.

He eased the bill into his pocket and made a sweeping motion with his hand. I had raised my heel as though to strike off the locks.

"No, no. You take away. I not want you to open it here. You take."

I was almost laughing at my foolishness. I couldn't even carry the thing and I told him so.

"All right. You wait. One piece silver and I get two boys to take to your home. Then you can open, not before."

One piece of silver and I'd be flat. And I didn't have any home to take it to. But the two coolies came, shivering, and placed two ropes about the box. Then they took a long pole and thrust it through the loops, placed the pole on their shoulders and lifted the chest between them.

I walked confidently away as though I knew my destination perfectly and the coolies trudged wearily after me, hiding their heads in their collars to thwart the wind and the stinging dust.

What a fool I was—three meaningless characters and a chest full of something which might prove very dangerous. A lot of bravado had been in the purchase. Perhaps I was trying to fool myself that I wasn't being hunted throughout the city.

But the purchase had given me one thing. It had made me laugh—and laughter had been forgotten in the last few hectic days of flight. Almost light-hearted, I strode along, boots ringing on the pavement, oblivious of the wind which tugged at me.

Chapter Two

THEN I noticed an odd phenomenon. I had turned several corners and had proceeded as though I had a destination in mind. Perhaps it had been habit. I had ridden down this street before.

I checked myself so hurriedly that the lead coolie bumped against my back. Of course I'd been down this street before. It led to the mansion of General Hseng!

All unwittingly I had marched sedately straight into the jaws of a trap. I stood for a moment aghast at myself. Then, once more, I laughed. Why not?

General Hseng was far to the north, in camp beyond the Wall. Was it likely that he would leave a squad of soldiers in his house? I thought not. Perhaps only a few servants were there. At any rate I couldn't stay out in the night to freeze. I had to go somewhere. And the searchers would hardly think of looking into the home of the general.

More confident than ever, I marched ahead. Maybe the chest was bringing me good luck after all.

The walls of the compound which contained General Hseng's house were high and frowning, enclosing an acre or two of carefully screened gardens and buildings. A passerby would never suspect the beauty contained within. "All for the family, nothing for the stranger," runs the Spanish phrase. It might well be applied to Chinese.

At the gate I looked for a sentry. The conical guard box was deserted. The gates were closed and locked. I looked through a slot and saw that the house was dark.

It was improbable that any soldiers were about, but I had to summon up considerable nerve to clang the bell. It tore the night apart with its clamor and then, as the pulsating throb faded, the wind came back into its own.

The coolies stood like good draft horses, patiently waiting. Where I went was nothing to them, judging by their half-hidden faces.

After a long pause, a footstep sounded within the compound. A lantern was thrust up to the level of a man's head, showing the thin, smooth face of a middle-class Chinese.

"An officer of the general," I said, without showing much but my mouth, "with a chest for the general."

He was evidently sleepy and easily convinced. He unfastened the chains and admitted us. He lifted the lantern again and with a startled gasp, opened his mouth to yell. He had recognized me.

The yell was stifled instantly, all his breath knocked out of him by the prodding muzzle of my .45. "Lead on to the house," I said.

He went, expecting a bullet at every step. He opened the doors of the vast one-story structure which served as a living room. It was cold within, musty as though it had not been occupied for a long time. The lantern made our shadows leap against the silken draperies which hung on the walls.

The servant hastily swept together charcoal on the hearth and kindled a brazier. The warmth of it was good. He lighted the candles on the table and then stood back, nervously waiting his sentence.

The two coolies came in and set the chest in the center of the floor. Then, without waiting to be warmed or even waiting for their pay, they started toward the door. I stopped them and gave them the silver coin.

I must have been dull-witted at the moment, anxious to get at the box; for I let them go. When they had closed the door behind them, I turned to the servant.

"Are there soldiers here?"

"No, captain."

"You know that I shoot very well?"

"Yes, captain."

"Then get me a glass of whiskey out of that cabinet and make yourself comfortable. I shall not tie you until I wish to sleep."

"Thank you, captain." He scurried to the cabinet and I turned my attention to the box.

The locks were very, very strong. I kicked them with my heel time after time without dislodging them. Some swords were on a board against the wall. I took a thick blade, intending to use it as a prize.

A moan filled the room and subsided. I stiffened and then smiled. The wind which still howled was making me jumpy. I started again toward the box.

It moved!

The servant chattered with fear and backed away. I took

a firm grip on my .45 and inserted the blade under a lock. It gave with a dry rasp, sifting Peking dust on the thick rug. The second came and then the third.

The moan sounded again and this time I knew it came from within the chest. I kicked the lid open and stood back, automatic leveled.

And there in the long chest I beheld the face of a white girl. She was beautiful. I saw that in the first shock of surprise. Her eyes were half open and her cheeks were gray with cold. Her silky yellow hair was tumbled about her head in waves of gold.

I thrust my hands under her shoulders and knees and bore her swiftly to a couch. Then I pulled the charcoal burner close to her so that she could get the warmth of it. I touched the rim of the whiskey glass to her lips and she swallowed convulsively.

Her hands were as clammy as death and her blue eyes were almost without luster. Although the chest had been padded with a blanket, I wondered that the cold had not killed her.

She was neatly dressed in blue sport clothes and their plainness cried their cost.

I rubbed her wrists and gave her another swallow of whiskey. The servant brought blankets and we wrapped her in them. I sat down, waiting for the warmth to take effect.

Almost fifteen minutes later, she started up suddenly and stared wildly about her. Then she saw me and interrogation replaced the fear in her eyes.

Her voice was throaty and she spoke with an accent which added to, rather than detracted from, her speech.

"Who are you? Where is this?"

I kicked the lid open and stood back, automatic leveled.
And there in the long chest I beheld the face of a white girl.
She was beautiful.

"You are in the house of General Hseng, the renowned savior of North China."

"That devil? God . . . Then you're one of his officers!"

"Lately one of his officers. Perhaps you have heard of the very despicable Captain Royal Sterling?"

Her face remained questioning. She had not heard of me and I was extremely glad of it.

"Unfortunately," I said, "General Hseng is away campaigning and is not here to receive you."

"But . . . but how did I get here?"

I pointed at the box. "You came in that. You see . . . er . . . well, that is, I bought you."

"Bought me?"

"Yes. And may I ask your name?"

"Sandra Kolita." She said it quietly, but as though it meant a great deal. The name Kolita stirred vague memories in the back of my head. Something about Mongolia, but I couldn't place my finger on it.

"From Mongolia?"

"Yes. But you haven't answered my question. How did I get here?"

"I haven't the faintest idea," I said. "You appear to have been slugged or drugged. What do you remember?"

"I . . . I don't remember the coffin," she replied. "Two men seized me at the North Gate and dragged me into a car. I . . . don't remember much after that. They . . ." Her calm broke and she fell back on the couch, covering her face with her arm.

I made her raise up and take another jolt of whiskey. The pupils of her eyes were dilated; drugged, I decided.

"But why should anyone place me in a chest?"

I shook my head. "All I know is that I bought you and the chest in the Thieves' Market. I'm sorry I dragged you into a mess like this, but it's better than waking up in the house of some merchant—the outside of which you'd never see again. I don't suppose they thought any foreign devils would be buying in the Thieves' Market on a night like this."

She was getting better by the second and I found myself admiring her vitality. Most any girl I had ever known would have been in bed for weeks after such exposure and drugging.

"How . . . how much did I cost?"

"Five Mex," I told her, very solemnly. "I had five Mex and a silver piece."

"All your money?"

"That's right."

"Then I must be very valuable to you."

"Perhaps you are, but let me assure you that whatever they say of me, I have never been called otherwise than a gentleman."

"I didn't mean that," she said, abashed.

"But see here. I'm not exactly shooting square with you. I'm on the run. I killed a man named Wu up north in self-defense; and as Mr. Wu seems very vital to the powers that be, I'm about to be shot as a murderer by the first firing squad I run across. There's the door. As soon as you are rested, beat it to your friends and forget that you ever heard of me. My friends are not exactly enviable."

"You're in . . . in a position like that and yet you spent your last cent on me?"

47

"I didn't know you were in the chest," I said, "so forget knight errantry."

"It doesn't matter," she replied, forgetting all about her own predicament in the face of mine. "You must do something. What are you doing in the house of General Hseng?"

"I had to spend the night someplace, didn't I?"

She laughed for a full minute and when she fell silent again her eyes were bright. She threw aside the blankets and stood up, shakily but greatly revived. She was tall and straight, about five feet six, and her slenderness suggested a life completely devoid of pink tea.

Warming her hands over the brazier she looked long at me, studying me. "You don't know who I am," she decided.

"Not exactly."

"As long as I'm your property now," she said, laughing, "perhaps I had better tell all. Sandra Kolita is the daughter of Kolita of Uliassutai."

Suddenly my mind clicked out the required information. I had heard Hseng speak longingly of several thousand acres of rich land hidden away north of the Gobi; of gold mines, timber and cattle. And Kolita owned the region—a land as big as a New England state.

Kolita was a White Russian, very proud, of ancient lineage which traced him back to the first rulers of the steppes, to the Vikings who at one time ruled Russia. He had come out of the Revolution with money and his life and had invested all of it in Mongolia, gathering in some of the finest land procurable in that otherwise desolate plateau.

"Gold mines," I said. "Enough men to form a large army—and who do. Yes, I've heard of Kolita of Uliassutai. Why would anyone attack his daughter?"

"I . . . I don't know."

I stood for a long time at her side, thinking. Then I frowned. "If you were found in the possession of anyone and that person had hidden you against your will, it would go hard with him. But if you just disappeared forever, then what would happen?"

"My father would come for me."

"Exactly. For some reason, somebody wants your father to leave his estates."

Her eyes shot wide with both surprise and fear. "You mean . . . I see. They would murder him when he was away from his men and then, without him to fight, it would be easy to take over his properties. Who would want to do that?"

"General Hseng, perhaps.

"They've sent word to him. Perhaps he is already on his way. But no, it would take some time to get to him. Communication is slow.

"The messenger," I said, "has twelve hours' start. It remains for us to beat him to your father."

"But you spent your last cent for me," she protested. "I have no money."

"No, but the general must have left a car. And I have several clips for this .45. We'll see what we can see and do what we can."

"But you're wanted for murder!"

"Exactly. Might as well leave by the north as any way."

I moved toward the door. A sound came to me—the throbbing of a motor.

Footsteps followed an instant later, many of them. A Chinese voice bawled, "He's in there! Surround the place!"

Those coolies! Of course I'd been followed from the club. No wonder they'd forgotten their pay.

I whirled on the servant who cowered away. "Where is the garage? Quick!"

"Through the front door," he chattered.

"That's blocked. Have you no other exit?" I helped his mind with the muzzle of the automatic. He ran toward the rear and parted a curtain there, displaying a flight of steps.

I hesitated only long enough to gather up an armful of blankets. I knew how cold it would be. Then, holding blankets and my .45, I hurried down the stairs, closely followed by Sandra and the unwilling servant. I knew my way about from here. I had often been in the general's garden. The garage was less than a hundred feet from the back of the house.

My boots crunched on the gravel of the drive. Men were shouting in the front of the house, their voices almost drowned in the whine of the gale. Sandra was beside me. We had lost the servant.

A blanket came loose and almost tripped me. I paused for an instant to gather in the loose end. The instant was fatal. A soldier rounded the end of the house. The light from a window fell upon his cap ornament and the gun he held.

Flame blotted out his silhouette. He was firing with a light machine gun!

Chapter Three

PAIN shot like lightning through me. My entire chest went numb. Jerked and hammered and turned, I fell hard to the gravel, unable to breathe. My hand was filled with sticky blood. My body was a hotbed of agony. I seemed to roll forever. There would be no end to this but death. For an eternity I was certain that I was about to die, that I had already been killed, that this was my last split second on earth.

The blurring flash from the light machine gun lighted up the enclosure. The soldier yelled triumphantly and charged forward. But, in spite of my iron-clad knowledge that I had been hit many, many times in the chest, a soldier's reflex took care of me. I raised the .45 without knowing that I did so. The muzzle spat once. The Chinese crumpled like a bag of meal.

I heard the garage doors squeal as they were opened. I heard many feet pounding toward me. But I could not move or breathe or even think.

Gradually my breath came back. I expected to taste blood but I did not. Something very odd was occurring. I had been hit by a dozen machine-gun slugs but I was still alive.

The knowledge gave me the will to fight on. The light

machine gun was less than a yard from my outstretched hand. I was working with a coolness I had experienced before but which had never become ordinary to me. Without any volition whatever, I pocketed the .45, crawled to my knees and leveled the light machine gun.

A powerful engine barked alive in the garage. Men ran across the lighted square by the house. I pressed the trigger and swept them with garish fire.

I was still expecting to momentarily fall over dead. But I kept telling myself that Sandra had to get out of this. It never occurred to me that these soldiers should have no interest in her.

Shadows and bright buttons fell away from me. Bayonets glittered as they fell. More men were coming.

A long phaeton swerved out of the garage. The headlights picked out the Chinese, held them stark against blackness. The gun battered my shoulder, rocked me as I knelt.

Sandra was behind the wheel. Above the roar of the engine, she cried, "Get in!"

I threw the blankets into the rear seat and vaulted over the door. Gears crashed. Men leaped away. The windshield splintered. Showered by flying glass, we careened toward the gate.

Three men were there, striving to close the iron gates. I fired with the wind biting my face. They melted aside.

We rounded the gate with a squeal of protesting rubber and streaked down the narrow *hutung* toward the North Gate and freedom.

STORIES *from the* GOLDEN AGE

☐ Yes, I would like to receive my **FREE CATALOG** featuring all 80 volumes of the *Stories from the Golden Age Collection* and more!

Name
_____

Shipping Address
_____

City _____ State _____ ZIP _____

Telephone _____ E-mail _____

Check other genres you are interested in: ☐ SciFi/Fantasy ☐ Western ☐ Mystery

FREE SHIPPING!
NO PURCHASE REQUIRED

6 Books • 8 Stories
Illustrations • Glossaries

6 Audiobooks • 12 CDs
8 Stories • Full color 40-page booklet

Fold on line and tape

- -

IF YOU ENJOYED READING THIS BOOK, GET THE ACTION/ADVENTURE COLLECTION **AND** SAVE 25%

BOOK SET
~~$59.50~~ $45.00
ISBN: 978-1-61986-089-6

AUDIOBOOK SET
~~$77.50~~ $58.00
ISBN: 978-1-61986-090-2

☐ Check here if shipping address is same as billing.

Name
_____

Billing Address
_____

City _____ State _____ ZIP _____

Telephone _____ E-mail _____

Credit/Debit Card #: _____

Card ID # (last 3 or 4 digits): _____

Exp Date: ____/____ Date (month/day/year): ____/____/____

Order Total *(CA and FL residents add sales tax)*: _____

To order online, go to: **www.GoldenAgeStories.com** or call toll-free **1-877-8GALAXY** or 1-323-466-7815

Gears crashed. Men leaped away. The windshield splintered.
Showered by flying glass, we careened toward the gate.

The car was a Benz, well-upholstered, well-built, designed for speed and hard wear. The top was down and the wind blasted at us, chilling us. Sandra drove fast and well. Her slippered foot was all the way down on the accelerator and her silky hair stood out behind her head like a Valkyrie's.

Peking fled away from us, wall by wall, street by street. No one tried to bar our way in the city, even though I knew phones would be jangling all about the seven walls, ordering out every soldier and officer in an effort to stop us.

I reached into the back seat for one of the blankets and felt a round pellet roll out of a fold. I pulled the covering to me and through it I could see the light of the dash. The thing was riddled.

Patting my chest gingerly I found that I was very bruised, but otherwise untouched. A scratch on my wrist accounted for the blood in my hand.

The blankets I had carried out of the house had acted as a perfect bulletproof vest, stopping the slugs sufficiently so that they could not pierce even my trench coat.

Sandra smiled at me and I smiled back. Good luck, long life and happiness. She was certainly bringing me two of those things and she might well bring me three.

The towers of the North Gate rose spectrally before us. The Benz roared through, bounced over railroad tracks and streaked for the open country.

The wind was colder. My face felt like sandpaper from the beating of the dust.

"Stop and wrap up in a blanket," I yelled in Sandra's ear.

She slowed down and applied the brake without turning

out of the road. I saw then that she was terribly tired from exposure and excitement and hard driving. The whiskey I had given her had worn away.

I got out and went around to the driver's side. From the back seat I took more blankets, all of them pierced but still serviceable, and swathed her in them until she looked like a butterfly in a cocoon.

Then I received a surprise. The back seat of the car was so fitted that it could be made into a short but comfortable berth. Evidently General Hseng had built this car to order. There were straps for binoculars and maps. And praise be, the maps were still there! —also the binoculars, a field compass and a flashlight!

I took the flash and examined my find in greater detail. A bright knob caught my eye and I pulled it out. A section of the front seat was lowered into a table: glasses glittered, packages of cigarettes, tins of food and last but not least, several varieties of brandy, whiskey and rum.

With a flourish, I poured four fingers of brandy into a glass, added a squirt of soda and handed it to Sandra. When I made one for myself, I presented mine to hers.

"Here's to Hseng," I said. "We've got everything but ice."

She shivered with mock severity and drank. I restored the glasses to the miniature bar and closed up shop for future reference. Then I looked around the car with the flash.

The tires and spares were in excellent shape. The gas tank was a tremendous thing, brimming full, holding close to ninety gallons.

When I saw that I began to wonder why this car was all equipped and ready for Hseng. He certainly didn't keep it that way all the time, especially since he had been away on campaign for months. What was this all about?

Puzzled I climbed under the wheel and we started out again. Sandra was quiet, thinking about her father, probably, worrying about whether or not we could beat the messenger to Uliassutai.

A glare of light flickered momentarily on the splintered windshield. I turned around and looked back. A pair of headlights were less than a mile behind us, dancing across the plain as though traveling fast.

The road we traveled had not been repaired since the Mings. It was marked by grave mounds and shrines and excavated paving blocks. But the Benz had been built for heavy work and I gave it all the gas it would take.

In spite of the swirling clouds of gray dust and the cold which made my eyes water, I could make out the North Star high above us. We were traveling in the right direction, a little to the west of it. Before dawn we'd make the Wall. And if we were lucky, we'd be heading into Inner Mongolia by daylight.

But the headlights behind were relentlessly closing the gap.

"Who is it?" said Sandra in my ear.

"The devil himself for all I know. Probably Hseng."

"You mean he's sore about stealing his car?"

"And about my killing Wu and about our using his house and about the theft of a vehicle he obviously had prepared for his own immediate use."

Sandra studied the headlights behind us as though they would answer the question. "He's gaining on us."

"I'm giving it all it will take."

Then Sandra thumped my arm excitedly. "There's another car behind the one following us."

"Follow the leader," I hazarded, "and while we've still got the edge on them, I'm going to do some leading."

The stabbing glare of our own lights caught a bridge railing and below that a dry wash which would be a swelling river during the rains. The bank was steep, strewn with rocks.

I clicked off the lights. Sandra gasped. It was an ugly sensation. We dived down the embankment, tires thundering over stones. By guess more than sight I yanked the wheel and braked, swinging us in under the bridge and, I hoped, out of sight.

"If you know any prayers," I told Sandra, "get them lined up."

I picked up the light machine gun, found a few bullets still in it and climbed out. The growing bellow of the pursuing machine was still far from us. I took down Hseng's bar and mixed us a couple quick ones in the cold dark. As Sandra drank, I heard her teeth rattle against the edge of the glass. It wasn't fear. It was honest cold.

Brakes screeched. The other machine was slowing down. Far behind it came two more glaring eyes. I knew then that they would certainly look under the bridge, knowing that we had turned off our lights and understanding that it was impossible to drive through the dark.

Nothing for it but to make a stand. I thrust the light machine gun on the planks over my head and swung myself up. I felt like Horatius himself. Sandra started our engine again and prepared for a hasty departure.

The headlights picked me out. The brakes squealed louder. A red flash of powder flame jabbed at me. The bullet yowled away from a rock.

They had asked for it. I leveled the machine gun and let drive, firing higher than their headlights. The car careened to one side, slammed off the road and skidded toward me sideways through a cloud of gray dust.

By the glare of their headlights I could see three men standing up, trying to get out. One was bulky, clutching a valise. That was Hseng.

All in a glance, I fired again, low this time. Above the blast of bullets I heard a tire explode.

Screams came from the machine, now less than twenty feet from me and broadside. The three men stayed still and elevated their hands. Hseng still clutched the valise. A split-second impression told me that one of the men was white.

Stiff-legged and jittery, I went forward. Hseng recognized me with a wail. That he was surprised came as a shock. Didn't he know whom he was trailing?

His face was like butter, his black, stringy mustache curved mournfully down on either side of his mouth.

"Captain Sterling!" whined Hseng.

I chucked the gun into the present arms and brought it back into position. "At your service, general. At your service."

"What are you doing here?" cried Hseng.

"What are *you* doing here, *general*?"

"I . . . I follow you, of course." He was blustering now, but he still held to the valise.

For an instant I had forgotten the other car. Now it made its presence known by skidding up beside Hseng's machine. An automatic rapped from the midst of a suddenly animated crowd of men.

Soldiers!

Chapter Four

I waited to see no more. A firing squad was once again beckoning with a bony finger. Before those others could swarm out of their truck, I began to fire. The automatic snapped back. A man with the general collapsed. Another ran blindly toward the wash, diving headlong out of sight under the bridge.

The noise was terrific. Rifles of every known make were adding their clamor to the chatter of the machine gun which bucked in my hands. A slug twitched my collar and I realized that I was in plain sight.

I threw myself down into the dust and propped the gun up on my elbows. These men were of Hseng's regiment—I gathered that much. They were about ten in number, all of them yelling at once.

Abruptly I missed Hseng. The yellow dog was taking a beat, leaving me here to cover his going. But he wouldn't get far on the plain in this bitter night.

Dust stung my face, thrown up by a rifle bullet. The soldiers were all on the ground now, trying to get up enough courage to stand and face the machine gun. I couldn't see very much beyond the flare of my weapon. I had to guess at the targets. Every time I stopped firing, red spots danced before my face to be immediately replaced by blackness. Hseng's machine was suddenly alive.

That was too much. I was flanked and outnumbered and to cap it, the bolt of the gun slammed home with an empty click.

Jumping to my knees I saw that a man was rushing me from the right. I threw the machine gun into his face and he fell back, stunned.

Taking the .45, I started to back away. I couldn't see the soldiers and now that I had stopped firing, they couldn't see me. It was an eerie sensation, death stalking me through the darkness.

Wait until I caught up with Hseng this time! I'll pretty up his face for him.

Walking backward, I neared the other end of the bridge. I could hear the Benz motor between shots from the truck and touring car. The soldiers were waiting to make certain of my position before they rushed. In the flash of their powder I saw their momentarily illumined silhouettes.

The uncertainty gnawed at me. I was unable to get back to the Benz without rushing the Chinese—and one man launching an attack was rather out of the question.

They decided matters for me. Their firing stopped. I heard a loud command, "Forward!"

Boots hammered the bridge planking like kettle drums. I was caught! Unable to retreat through the darkness, charged by yelling Chinese, held in the gleam of a flashlight, I mentally kissed Sandra goodbye and shook my own hand in farewell.

But I had counted without Sandra. With a snarl, the Benz roared out of the wash and leaped up my side of the embankment. Or was it Sandra? I caught a hasty glimpse of bulky shoulders bent over the wheel as the machine roared toward me.

It was going about fifteen on the upgrade. I sprinted toward the spot it would climb out. The Chinese pack yelled at my heels.

One hand on the door, one foot on the running board, the air sliced at me as the car gathered speed.

For one foolish instant I thought I was safe. Then a gun blasted at me, singeing my face. The driver of the car had fired straight up.

The barrel of my automatic was sufficient. I brought it down. It didn't bounce. It stayed there. The driver fell away from the wheel. The Benz swerved toward a gaping ditch. A shot from the rear cut a gash in the steel side just under my clutching hand.

Snatching the wheel, I pulled the machine back in the road. Tossing a foot over the side, I kicked the man's body out of the way and down to the floor. Then I slid under and tramped on the accelerator.

Those behind were not attempting to follow. Hseng's car was out of commission and the truck was too slow. I turned my attention to the men who had pirated the machine—and not an instant too soon.

Braking, I turned to look in the back seat, afraid that Sandra had been left behind. Hseng reared up and his gun was shaking in his hand. He had not dared to shoot me while I was driving. He was too far from the wheel. But now he could complete the job he had started.

The Benz stopped. I saw Hseng level his automatic. I was certain that my last moment on earth was here at last. And then a white hand lashed out and knocked the gun and the blasting shot aside.

Before Hseng could direct the muzzle again, I leaped over the back of the front seat and slammed a good, hard right into his jaw. His mustache seemed to curl up at the points as he fell back.

Sandra freed herself of the arm Hseng had used to hold her down. Very white of face in the feeble reflection of the dashlight, but she nevertheless solemnly reached out and took my hand.

Together we laughed. It was hysteria, of course, but the laugh helped us.

"They came down the bank and mobbed me," said Sandra. "I couldn't do a thing. But then, you did enough, so it's all right."

"If you're all right."

"I'm fine. Who are these gentlemen? Friends of yours?"

"The very best," I assured her.

Taking the flashlight I looked at the man I had hit with the barrel of my gun.

Compton!

Frederick Compton wasn't dead, but he was very numb. His thick fur cap had saved his skull. I didn't know whether I was sorry or not.

As for Hseng, he was only temporarily out. Sandra pushed him to one side and wrapped a blanket tightly about him. We tied the blanket and Hseng all in one piece, using tire chains and tape.

Compton received the same treatment and the tow rope. We placed them together and let them finish their enforced slumber. Then we had a drink and proceeded to investigate the bag Hseng had held so tightly.

Once more we were due for a surprise. The flash fell on newspaper-size Bank of Taiwan bills, green American money and British pound notes.

Sandra gasped. "I've never seen so much money all together in my life. There must be a million dollars here!"

I rummaged deeper through the crisp, new currency. Then I brought the traitors to light. Yen notes—Japanese money. So that was Hseng's game.

The defender of the North had sold out. He had stood for years between the Japanese and Peking. Now the Japanese could have the town. Hseng had sold out.

"Stuffed shirt," I said with contempt. I said a great many things more, all of them unprintable.

It was like a poker hand suddenly called and turned face up on the table. Everything fitted and made a full house. And right then I thought I was holding four aces.

"You know who boxed you up?" I said.

Sandra shook her head.

"Hseng."

Her eyes widened.

"Hseng has no place to go," I said. "Russia wouldn't harbor

65

him. He couldn't get through the coast. He had to take Mongolia or nothing. And the best land in Mongolia belongs to your father. Therefore, Hseng had you caught when you arrived in Peking. He intended to drag your father away by that ruse."

Sandra was quick to grasp it. "Then he still has troops. His men are somewhere between Kalgan and Uliassutai. They'll stop Dad, hold him until Hseng joins them, perhaps kill him and proceed to Uliassutai. Once there they'll overpower the leaderless troops of my father and take everything."

"We'd better be going," I said, thinking of fifteen hundred miles between Peking and Uliassutai—and the not-to-be-ignored Gobi.

I climbed under the wheel and sent the Benz streaking over the rough road toward Kalgan on the Great Wall, the start of an ancient caravan route into the depths of Inner and Outer Mongolia.

Kolita alone could save me—and Kolita was walking straight into some of Hseng's troops far to the north. Under Kolita's protection, I could literally give the bird to Chinese politicians. If I missed connections, I could go nowhere. Russia would strengthen her friendship with China by seeing that I was handed over to Chinese authorities without delay. Kolita alone could put a stop to that.

And Liang-Tsi-Wu. Where had he fit in? Why had he tried to kill me? The answer was riding in the back seat. Hseng must have told him a lie about something I had said, thereby egging Wu to provoke a quarrel with me. Hseng knew I'd shoot Wu and I did. Wu would have prevented

Hseng's final sellout. Wu was the fly in Hseng's tea. And Captain Royal F. Sterling, with his customary brain power, had accommodatingly shot Wu for Hseng.

At first I had been a sidelight on the general scheme, but I was making my presence felt now. How things would turn out, I did not know. Hseng's pick of his regiment was waiting somewhere ahead, anywhere, watching the caravan route both ways. If only Kolita had not started—but then, it was a fifty-fifty shot that Kolita would be killed by Hseng's men the instant they laid hands on him.

Black thoughts sent us hurtling through the black night. I did not notice the cold now. I was burning up with excitement. This was a race against an intangible thing—a problematical occurrence. I had no way of knowing what would happen, what I should do about it if it did.

Sandra clutched my arm. "I just thought . . . There's a radio at Uliassutai!"

It was the last straw. Kolita would have received the message already. Perhaps he was already dead, and if he was, then Captain Royal F. Sterling would soon be talking the matter over with him in a place considerably warmer than the wintery plains of North China.

Chapter Five

A Mongol horseman, many years ago, made the fifteen-hundred-mile trip from Uliassutai across the Gobi to Peking. He made it in eight days, changing horses every fifteen miles at the post stations provided for that purpose.

By noon, I knew that if Kolita had received the radio in morning of the day before, he would be twenty-four hours on his way. He would want to make time and therefore he would be practically alone, driving a fast car. It was conceivable that he had already completed one third of the journey or five hundred miles.

If we didn't meet Hseng's troops first, then at midnight we should expect to meet Kolita.

Compton was sullen. I had offered to unlash him if he promised to be decent about it, but he preferred the role of martyr and he shivered in the blanket, bound by the tow rope. Hseng was quite willing to promise anything. Something of the buttery look had gone from his face. He was plainly scared. But a man who would sell out his country was certainly able to sell out on a mere promise; and so, Hseng also shivered and ate dust.

At dark we stopped at Borbo, a squalid, lifeless whistling post on the old caravan trail, well into the bitter Gobi and

Outer Mongolia. Thousands of square miles of trackless, gravelly waste was on every side, relieved only by the flattopped, dreary looking ranges in the distance.

Kolita kept a store of gasoline here for his own personal use and Sandra convinced the aged Mongol keeper that it was quite all right to give us fuel. We filled our mammoth tanks and prepared to go on.

Sandra thought of something else. She asked the Mongol, "Have any soldiers passed this point recently, heading north?"

Hseng sat up as well as he could, his eyes drilling the Mongol.

"Yes," replied the aged one. "Three days past many men came in trucks. They were . . ." he spat with distaste at the words, "Chinese and Manchurians."

"Three days?" I said.

He nodded and went back into his hut and the sheep dung fire which smoldered odorously there. We drove on, Sandra at the wheel.

"So," I said to Hseng, "you weren't sure where your men are."

"Oh, no!" said Hseng.

"And you, Compton, know nothing about any of this."

"Why ask me?" growled Compton, his puffy face apathetic.

"Then," I said to Sandra, "we drive with all speed but with great caution. I do not think they would go closer than five hundred miles to Uliassutai. The country gets settled there."

An hour later, bumping over rocks, following the indistinct trail, I spotted a dot of red in the distance.

"The fools!" snapped Hseng, suddenly angry.

"Thanks," I said.

Sandra, using her knowledge of the way, turned from the trail and headed toward the cold shadows of the mountains to our right. We proceeded for some time without lights. I had lost sight of the campfire.

Sandra stopped. "Over this ridge, you'll see their camp. I'll stay here and look after our prisoners. Two make twice as much noise."

Climbing out, I gathered my coat about me and hefted my .45. As an afterthought I took the valise full of money Hseng had extracted from the Japanese.

Sandra's hand was on my sleeve as though unwilling to let me go. Her grip tightened and she dragged me back to her. Her face was a vague, soft blur in the darkness. "Don't . . . don't let anything happen to you."

The shock of her kiss made my hand tremble. Resolutely, I turned away and headed for the ridge above us.

From the summit, I could see the camp spread out before me. There were many men there, all of them from the old 20th. They had driven their trucks into a circle to protect them from the sweeping wind. A leaping fire burned in the enclosure.

I gave a start. A man was sitting before the blaze, but his position was unnatural. He was tied. Kolita!

What I wouldn't have given for a machine gun or a mountain battery. But my .45 would have to suffice. The machine gun was empty. If I could sneak down to their camp without being seen, I would be able to get Kolita free—with several tons of luck.

Starting down the slope, I was arrested by a high-pitched shout behind me. Something had happened at the car!

Sprinting back, I heard other shouts and then all was ominously quiet. I had to do something, and I certainly wouldn't help my case by walking straight into their hands. I slowed down.

The car lights were blazing. Across them marched the silhouettes of soldiers. I knew then that they had spotted us out on the plain and had kept us in sight through night glasses.

Hseng's twangy voice came to me above the clatter of guns and the stamp of ponies. "Captain Sterling is down by your camp. You know him. You know that he is a murderer. Get him!"

A strange voice said, "What shall we do with this woman?"

"Take her to the camp. She is a spy."

There came a pause and then a startled exclamation from Hseng. "The money! The money is gone!"

Men scurried about, hauling everything out of the car. I could see Sandra held by two soldiers. She watched clear-eyed and unafraid. I knew then the confidence she had in me.

"Sterling has it!" cried Hseng. "Hunt him down and shoot him on sight!"

I could do no good here. I moved along the ridge until I was out of their path, and watched them depart. I had no illusions about my own fate. These soldiers were the dregs of the regiment. Hseng had bought them with promises of loot, leaving the better men to take the brunt of the Japanese invasion.

After they had gone, I cautiously followed them. A man had been left on guard at the car. The camp was in an uproar. Men were scurrying in every direction, poking through everything in an effort to find me, jabbing their naked bayonets into piles of fodder and stacks of blankets.

Someway, I had to release Kolita and Sandra. I could hardly expect to do it by force.

A hundred yards away from the camp I saw a shadow pass between myself and the fire. A man was close to me. On top of one of the trucks I saw the silhouette of a soldier sitting behind a machine gun.

Suddenly a face loomed in front of me. It was an officer, coat collar upturned, saber in his hand. I could see the glint in his eyes, as hard and merciless as the shimmer of his upraised blade.

I heard the whistle of steel as the sword came down. By guess rather than skill, I caught the blow on the barrel of my .45. He was too startled to cry for aid. Before he could recover his sword, I slammed him on the head with the muzzle of my gun. He crumpled, striking the toe of my boot as he went down.

In the next half minute, I changed coats and caps with him. Then, summoning up my nerve, I yelled for the men.

They came streaming toward me through the darkness. They had neither lanterns nor flashlights. The first one to arrive bumped squarely into me, utterly unable to make me out.

I pointed mutely at the officer's body. The man did the rest. He roared, "The captain!"

Men ran faster toward us. The soldier was hauling at the body, dragging it toward the fire. Every one began to jabber at once, every soldier tried to help drag the unfortunate Chinese toward the trucks.

I preceded them. Men slammed against me without paying

me any heed whatever. They were too interested in the cries out front. Expecting to be recognized and shot down at any moment, I made my way slowly ahead, trying not to hurry, as though I led the triumphal parade.

But my luck was not holding. The sentry on top of the truck had not deserted his machine gun as I had intended he should in the excitement. I reached the tail gate and climbed slowly up on it. The firelight struck me full in the face. I didn't know him but he knew me. His slant eyes were suddenly shot with terror. He strove to slew his weapon about.

In the split second which followed, the machine gun started up and I fired. The gun stopped in the same breath. The sentry sagged over the breech and then into the bottom of the truck, drilled between the eyes.

Silence followed from the crowd on the plain. I could not see them, but I could sense their gaping paralysis. I turned the machine gun toward them, ready to let drive. Then I raised my voice and cried:

"Any man who wants to live, let him come and place his rifle by the fire. For that he will receive one thousand dollars Mex. Any man who wants to fight, let him fight. I am ready."

They knew me. For a full minute no man moved. They could see me clearly and, in their amazement, they never stopped to think that I could not see them at all, backed as they were by the dense blackness of the Gobi.

I was afraid of men still in the camp. I froze when I heard something grate on the truck side. Then I gasped with relief.

Sandra, rifle in hand, slid up over the side and faced the fire. "All right, my captain," she said in a businesslike voice.

An instant later Kolita came and I knew that she had waited to untie him. Kolita was tall and gaunt and white-bearded, and his pale blue-eyes were mad clear through.

"Shoot the so-and-sos," snapped Kolita, crisply.

Hseng's treachery turned the trick. Hseng bawled, "Charge! He has no money! He lies! Kill him."

And there at my side was the valise crammed with dollars. But no one thought to argue about it.

Kolita was clutching a flare-snouted machine gun. He smiled without any humor whatever.

"Duck!" I yelled.

Chapter Six

THE Chinese were in motion. Their feet hammered the hard-packed plain, their voices rose in a terrifying discord. They fired as they ran. Bullets rained splinters from the sides of the truck.

The machine gun started up, spraying red flame far away from me. Kolita, kneeling at my side, added his weapon to the clamor. Sandra still faced the campfire. Her rifle rapped with the steady regularity of a well-trained soldier's.

We had no targets out front but the flash of rifles and the occasional lesser sparkle of an ornament. The Chinese were not running so fast now. They were trying to form some kind of order. I swore at myself for all those days I had spent on the rifle range, making decent shots out of them.

My cap went spinning and I crouched lower. It seemed to me that the glow from the rear was growing less. Then I knew what Sandra was using for a target. She was putting out the fire, shot by shot.

Sandra's rifle stopped and for a heart-frozen instant I thought she had been hit. By the belching flame from Kolita's machine gun I saw that she was gone.

Puzzled, I went back to the machine gun.

A moment later, the truck's headlights went on. Then the next and the next until every one in the circle was lit.

The plain was alight. It reminded me of a carnival and I half expected to hear the ballyhoo artist deliver his spiel. But this carnival was attended only by death.

I stopped firing long enough to lower some of the side boards on the outward side of the truck. Our heads were no longer in silhouette.

And still no Sandra. I began to be worried about her. Perhaps she had been hit while exposing herself in the headlights. A metallic rattle came to me an instant later. Sandra climbed over the side and dropped down. She was carrying an armload of belts for the machine gun.

"Orders, my captain," said Sandra.

"This begins to look like your war," I said above the machine gun's clamor.

"I am trying to make it mine," said Kolita.

The men out front were falling back, preparing for one last charge. I could see the huddled bodies on the plain and knew that our fire had been effective. I listened for Hseng's voice while I reloaded. It did not come. Maybe he was dead.

The soldiers were spreading out, trying to surround us.

An automatic roared close at hand. Kolita gasped and I thought he was hit. A soldier was on top of the truck next in line. Kolita swung his machine gun sideways and fired. The man's face disappeared. His body slithered down over the radiator and to the ground.

Sandra was gone again. I looked hurriedly about without finding her. Sweet, gallant Sandra. I wished she wouldn't be so energetic.

Kolita's fine, strong face was grimed with powder smoke.

A soldier was on top of the truck next in line.
Kolita swung his machine gun sideways and fired.
The man's face disappeared.

He looked sideways at me and gave me a flash of white teeth. It came over me that he was actually enjoying himself.

To my gun-deafened ears, the sound of a motor came as a shock. Before I had time to brace myself, the truck started ahead with a clash of gears.

For an instant I thought Sandra was running away from the camp. It was an excellent idea and I wholeheartedly seconded the move. I put the machine gun up on top of the cab and when the headlights picked out scurrying soldiery, I let them have it.

It was like hunting rabbits in the West, for a moment. I thought Sandra must be trying to run them down and then again I was wrong.

We headed out in the direction of Peking. I held on tight as the truck gathered speed and thundered along. I pounded on the cab and yelled, "No! You're going the wrong way!"

I saw Sandra's face for a moment. Sandra was smiling as her father had smiled. Fighting thoroughbreds they were, both of them. Sandra pointed briefly straight ahead.

Not until then did I see the two running figures far across the desert. Hseng and Compton!

We were not long in catching up with them. Sandra slowed down and I placed a racketing burst at their heels. They stopped, sagging with weariness, and turned apathetic eyes on us. We drew closer.

Hseng looked like he had melted, though it was close to zero. Compton was thoroughly whipped.

"Going someplace?" I asked. "It's a long run to Peking. Better get in, gentlemen, and hitch yourself a ride."

Walking with leaden feet, they came around to the back of the truck and stepped up, dropping to the floor, worn out.

"You said," I told them, "that I didn't have any money back there. Well, here's the valise. I haven't counted it yet, but I suspect the amount will knock you dead, Compton."

Compton didn't even glare. Sandra headed back toward the circle of car lights which marked the camp. The soldiers, astounded at our return, stood about in tight huddles, undecided whether to shoot or let us approach. Their reluctance to start a second war was undoubtedly due to the diminishing number of them.

Fifty yards from them, I stood up and called out, "We have General Hseng with us. If you care to fight, the machine guns are ready. If you want to save your lives, let us come closer."

They had nothing to say, and Sandra drove the truck ahead in low. When they were all within easy speaking distance, I said, "General Hseng sold out to the Japanese."

They evidently had an inkling of that, for their expressions did not change.

"General Hseng," I continued, "just now ran away from you, leaving you to take the brunt of our fire. He ran because he received more money from the Japanese than you think. He received one million dollars for China."

They stared at that. Compton gasped, "What the hell did you say?"

"I said he received one million dollars for China."

Compton's energy returned. He bounded up and seized Hseng by the throat. "You double-crossing fool! You . . ."

The Chinese, looking angry now, crowded up close to the

sides of the truck. They were not at all interested in us and I let them come.

"What's wrong?" I asked Compton.

"He . . . Oh, the fool. Japan bought him out, yes. But he was supposed to be acting for Japan now. If he hadn't severed all connection with them, they wouldn't give him any such sum as a million Mex. That's five hundred thousand gold, man! He's double-crossed me, double-crossed these men. He was supposed to split fifty-fifty and my cut was only forty thousand dollars."

I translated that for the benefit of the soldiers. They drew nearer, sullen as waiting tigers.

"Where do you fit in here?" I asked Compton.

"Oh, hell, there's no use being a goat twice."

"If you tell me, maybe I can save your neck."

Compton saw the logic of that. Kolita urged him by moving the machine-gun muzzle ever so little.

"Japan was supposed to give Hseng a bribe to leave the frontier open. Then they were going to commission Hseng—according to Hseng—as a general in their service. He was to push the Japanese arms closer toward Russia through Outer Mongolia. But Hseng lied. I wondered when no Japanese came to me, and when we met none on the road. He sold out his whole army, guns, men and horses—and received cash.

"I was supposed to be the go-between with commerce and foreign powers. We were to take Kolita's outfit in his absence. I knew nothing of this scheme to get Kolita away.

Then, from there, we were to organize armed bands and bring Mongolia under our hand. We were to set up another puppet empire right next to Russia. For my support, I was to receive one half of the bribe, all trading rights to the region where foreign commerce was concerned and was to receive the post of Minister of Commerce.

"But . . . but this fool! He intended to take most of the money. Oh, yes, you did, Hseng. And you intended to take over nothing more than Kolita's lands. Then you'd kill me, get another lot of men and go off entirely independent of Japan. You never were offered a generalship by Japan. You just dragged me in this so that you could make it look all right to the trading firms. Otherwise, they would have stopped you and would have dropped the noose over Japan's neck for buying you and your forces and leaving the northern frontier totally unprotected. If Japan knew that—boy, what wouldn't they do to you. They just thought you'd light out. You fool—as though you ever could have become the ruler of Mongolia . . ."

Kolita smiled and with a very matter-of-fact tone, told the soldiers all about it. They had been willing as long as they thought Japan was behind them, but when they saw their few numbers opposing all of Mongolia—

They crowded in closer. I waved them back.

"I do not like men who turn traitor," I said. "Neither do I like men who run away and leave their troops to fight. I would not kill Hseng if I were you." I paused for a moment for effect and then said, "I'd take him back to Manchuria and hand him over to the Imperial Japanese Army."

83

Hseng yowled for mercy, but Kolita and I picked him up and dropped him over the side. Soldiers gripped his arms, holding him. Compton looked sideways at me. "Do you think there's a reward for him?" he asked.

I turned my back on him and picked up the machine gun. Sandra got back under the wheel and we moved off toward the place we had left the Benz. None of the soldiers tried to follow us. The machine gun looked too authoritative and with Kolita's pale-blue eye along the sights, promised them much.

When we reached the Benz, we left the truck and climbed in. I started the machine down the slope, avoiding both the camp and the trail. Soon we were heading out toward Uliassutai and a land where there were meadows and lakes and mines, and where the word of Kolita was law.

Kolita, sitting in the back seat, slapped my arm as much as to say, "Good work."

"Who are you?" he asked.

"Captain Royal Sterling, late of the 20th Route. I might mention, sir, that I am at present wanted for murder in Peking."

"Ah," said Kolita, the wind whipping his white hair, "then you're as good with other weapons as you are with a machine gun. That is splendid. We have a little trouble up our way now and then, captain. Nothing so much—bandits, wandering Russian renegades—just enough to keep one from growing stale and too contented."

"Sir," I said, racing along over the uneven Gobi, heading almost due west, "before the night gets too far gone, let me ask you—" I stopped, not knowing how to continue.

He slapped my shoulder again. Sandra edged a little closer to me with a sigh.

"Of course, my captain," breathed Sandra. "Why, haven't you bought me already? Nicely boxed and everything?"

I liked Kolita when he laughed. "That's splendid, captain. I always wanted to keep my holdings in the family, so to speak."

We drove for quite a while after that and then, satisfied that we were not followed and that everything was well, I stopped and we lowered Hseng's portable bar and had us three drinks on the occasion.

I was getting back in when my hand struck the valise. I stopped, surprised. "Why . . . why, good God, we've still got that million Mex!"

And I recalled the characters on the chest and the three dogs with nine tails apiece. "Good luck! Long life! Happiness!"

Story Preview

Story Preview

NOW that you've just ventured through some of the captivating tales in the Stories from the Golden Age collection by L. Ron Hubbard, turn the page and enjoy a preview of *Spy Killer*. Join Kurt Reid, a man falsely accused of murder and grand larceny, who flees to Shanghai. After rescuing a White Russian spy, he's captured by the Chinese and forced into the cloak-and-dagger world of espionage and intrigue, where everything and everyone are not what they appear to be.

Spy Killer

THE water was black and the swim was long, but when a man is faced with death he does not consider odds.

Kurt Reid went over the side of the tanker *Rangoon* in a clean dive, cleaving the swirling dark surface of the Huangpu. The strong current swept him downriver toward the gaily lighted Bund. He did not want to go there. He knew that authorities would be after him like baying hounds before the night was out.

A shadow came between his half-immersed head and the glow. A sampan was sailing quietly through the gloom, its sculling oar stirring the thick black river.

Kurt Reid gripped the gunwale and slid himself over to the deck. The boatman stared at him with shuddering terror. Was this some devil come to life from the stream's depths?

"Ai! Ai!"

Kurt Reid was not too tired to grin. He stood up, water cascading from his black clothes.

"Put me ashore in the native city," he ordered in the Shanghai dialect.

"Ai . . . ai . . ."

"And chop-chop," added Kurt.

The boatman shriveled up over his oar. His eyes were two

saucers of white porcelain, even his coolie coat sagged. He put the small craft about and drove it swiftly in toward the bank.

Kurt Reid grinned back at the looming hulk of the *Rangoon*. He raised his hand in a mock salute and muttered, "Get me if you can, gentlemen." He turned then and faced the nearing shore.

As he wrung the water from his clothes he discarded his memories one by one. As mate of the *Rangoon*, he had been known as a bucko sailor, a hard case who struck first and questioned afterward, renowned for a temper as hot and swift as a glowing rapier.

And the reputation had not helped him when the captain had been found dead in his cabin and when it was discovered that the safe was open and empty. Kurt Reid had been the last man to see the captain alive, so they thought.

Shanghai stretched before him, and behind it lay all of China. If he could not escape there, he thought, he deserved to die. His only regret now was the lack of money he had been accused of stealing. A man does not go far on a few American dollars.

But, unlike most American mates, Kurt Reid had been raised in the Orient and he knew the yellow countries and their languages. Although his quick temper had earned his many enemies among the Japanese and Chinese, he hoped to avoid them. By now several men would be advised of his arrest and before morning his escape would also be known. Many men would think that excellent news and hope that his apprehension would be speedy.

If necessary he could assume one disguise or another. His eyes were the color of midnight and his hair was even blacker, and the pallor of his face could be easily made saffron.

The sampan rasped against a float and Kurt Reid, throwing a coin to the boatman, stepped ashore into the din of the native city.

Rickshaws clanged, vendors yowled their wares, jugglers threw tops high into the air and made them scream. Silk gowns rubbed against cotton gowns, scabby slippers stubbed over jeweled shoes. The crowds in the curving streets blended into the democracy of China.

Kurt Reid, head and shoulders above the rest, shoved his way toward a tea house. There, he supposed, he could dry his clothing and get himself a drink or two. Confidently he picked his way, looking neither to the right or the left, paying little heed to those who stopped to stare at this black-clothed giant who left the cobblestones spotted with his dripping passage.

The tea house was set a little apart from the other structures which hung flimsily over the street. The tea house had curving corners to foil the devils and a floating banner or two in red letters and a whole row of paper lanterns.

Kurt entered and rolled back the clouds of blue smoke which hung between ceiling and floor. Black caps bobbed, gowns rustled. Tea cups remained suspended for seconds.

Kurt went to the back of the room and found the round-faced, slit-eyed proprietor. "I want to dry my clothes. I fell into the river."

The man opened up a small cubicle at the rear, clapped his hands sharply, and presently a charcoal brazier was placed on the floor.

Kurt shut the door and disrobed, hanging his black flannel shirt and his bell-bottom pants over a bench to dry. Tea was brought, but he waved it aside in favor of hot rice wine.

The clothes began to steam and the rice wine took the chill from his body.

All unsuspecting and feeling at ease, Kurt began to plan ways and means of getting into the interior and away from possible arrest.

If he could buy a gown from this Chinese and perhaps a few other things, everything would be all right. He could join some party of merchants and get away.

But his plans were for nothing. His clothing was soon dry and he dressed again, feeling cheered and optimistic. He clapped his hands for the proprietor, and when that worthy came, Kurt was startled by a woman who sat with her back to the wall, staring out into the milling street.

Kurt slipped a dollar bill into the proprietor's hand. He still studied the woman. She was obviously a Russian. Her face was flat, with high cheekbones, and her nostrils were broad. There was the slightest hint of a slant to her eyes. She wore a coat made of expensive fur, and a small fur hat sat rakishly on the side of her blonde head. It was not usual to find Russian women alone in the native city, especially Russian women who dressed so well.

"Who is that?" demanded Kurt.

The Chinese inspected the girl as though he were seeing her for the first time. "Name Varinka Savischna," he replied, stumbling over the unfamiliar vowels of the Russian name.

"But . . . a white woman in the native city . . ." said Kurt.

"Russian woman," grumbled the Chinese. "She brings trouble to me." He looked at Kurt's lean body and handsome, inquisitive face and then grinned.

To find out more about *Spy Killer* and how you can obtain your copy, go to www.goldenagestories.com.

Glossary

Glossary

STORIES FROM THE GOLDEN AGE *reflect the words and expressions used in the 1930s and 1940s, adding unique flavor and authenticity to the tales. While a character's speech may often reflect regional origins, it also can convey attitudes common in the day. So that readers can better grasp such cultural and historical terms, uncommon words or expressions of the era, the following glossary has been provided.*

ballyhoo artist: someone who uses exaggerated or lurid material in order to gain public attention.

bucko: a person who is domineering and bullying.

Bund: the word *bund* means an embankment and "the Bund" refers to a particular stretch of embanked riverfront along the Huangpu River in Shanghai that is lined with dozens of historical buildings. The Bund lies north of the old walled city of Shanghai. This was initially a British settlement; later the British and American settlements were combined into the International Settlement. A building boom at the end of the nineteenth century and beginning of the twentieth century led to the Bund becoming a major financial hub of East Asia.

Forbidden City: a walled enclosure of central Peking, China, containing the palaces of twenty-four emperors in the Ming (1364–1644) and Qing (1644–1911) dynasties. It was formerly closed to the public, hence its name.

forty-five or **.45 automatic:** a handgun chambered to fire a .45-caliber cartridge and that utilizes the recoil or part of the force of the explosive to eject the spent cartridge shell, introduce a new cartridge, cock the arm and fire it repeatedly.

G-men: government men; agents of the Federal Bureau of Investigation.

Gobi: Asia's largest desert, located in China and southern Mongolia.

gunwale: the upper edge of the side of a boat. Originally a gunwale was a platform where guns were mounted, and was designed to accommodate the additional stresses imposed by the artillery being used.

Horatius: legendary Roman hero. He held an opposing army at bay while the Romans cut down a bridge connecting Rome with the road westward, thus preventing the enemy from crossing.

Huangpu: long river in China flowing through Shanghai. It divides the city into two regions.

hutung: (Chinese) a lane or alley.

ideographs: written symbols that represent an idea or object directly, rather than by particular words or speech sounds, as Chinese or Japanese characters.

Inner Mongolia: an autonomous region of northeast China. Originally the southern section of Mongolia, it was annexed by China in 1635, later becoming an integral part of China in 1911.

International Settlement: a reserved area in China set aside by the government where foreigners were permitted to reside and trade. These areas, called settlements or concessions, were leased from the Chinese government and were administered by the foreign residents and their consuls and not under the jurisdiction of Chinese laws or taxes. All such foreign settlements on mainland China were eventually dismantled when the Communist Party of China took control of the government in 1949.

Kalgan: a city in northeast China near the Great Wall that served as both a commercial and a military center. Kalgan means "gate in a barrier" or "frontier" in Mongolian. It is the eastern entry into China from Inner Mongolia.

legation: the official headquarters of a diplomatic minister.

light out: to leave quickly; depart hurriedly.

Manchuria: a region of northeast China comprising the modern-day provinces of Heilongjiang, Jilin and Liaoning. It was the homeland of the Manchu people, who conquered China in the seventeenth century, and was hotly contested by the Russians and the Japanese in the late nineteenth and early twentieth centuries. Chinese Communists gained control of the area in 1948.

Mex: Mexican peso; in 1732 it was introduced as a trade coin with China and was so popular that China became one of its principal consumers. Mexico minted and exported pesos to China until 1949. It was issued as both coins and paper money.

Morrison Street: street in Peking named after Australian George Morrison (1862–1920), a journalist and political advisor to the Chinese government. The street was the center for commercial activities.

Native Quarter: Native City; walled portion of the city where the native Chinese resided, also referred to as the Walled City. Foreigners in Tientsin lived in the International Settlement, located outside the Native City.

Outer Mongolia: originally the northern section of Mongolia, it was a political division of the Beiyang (warlord) Government, a series of military regimes that ruled from Peking from 1912 to 1928. Today the name is sometimes still informally used referring to Mongolia, a sovereign state, which controls roughly the same territory.

Peking: now Beijing, China.

phaeton: a vintage car body style, similar to a sedan or convertible sedan, where the rear-seat area is extended for added leg room, giving the vehicle the appearance that it is meant to be chauffeur-operated. This body type was popular up to the early years of World War II.

pink tea: formal tea, reception or other social gathering usually attended by politicians, military officials and the like.

pitch torch: a torch that was made by pounding a stick to loosen the fibers and then covering it with melted pitch until it was thoroughly soaked. When the pitch was hardened, another layer was spread thickly over it. This made a torch that burned brightly for many hours.

present arms: a position in which a long gun, such as a rifle, is held perpendicularly in front of the center of the body.

rapier: a small sword, especially of the eighteenth century, having a narrow blade and used for thrusting.

Route Army: a type of military organization exercising command over a large number of divisions. It was a common formation in China but was discarded after 1938.

sampan: any of various small boats of the Far East, as one propelled by a single oar over the stern and provided with a roofing of mats.

Scheherazade: the female narrator of *The Arabian Nights,* who during one thousand and one adventurous nights saved her life by entertaining her husband, the king, with stories.

shut of: free of; rid of.

slew: to turn about an axis; pivot.

Taku: site of forts built in the 1500s to defend Tientsin against foreign invasion. The forts are located by the Hai River, thirty-seven miles (60 km) southeast of Tientsin.

thirty-eight or **.38:** a .38-caliber pistol.

Tientsin: seaport located southeast of Peking; China's third largest city and major transportation and trading center. Tientsin was a "Treaty Port," a generic term used to denote Chinese cities open to foreign residence and trade, usually the result of a treaty.

tiger whiskers: whiskers from a tiger used in traditional remedies believed to cure ailments ranging from toothache to epilepsy; sold in markets in China.

Tom and Jerry glass: a thick glass for a hot drink called "Tom and Jerry," containing rum, brandy, nutmeg and egg, to which milk is sometimes added.

Uliassutai: at the time of the story, Outer Mongolia was divided into two administrative divisions: Uliassutai, which housed a military governor controlling the western division, and Urga, which housed the Chinese imperial agent who ruled the eastern division. Today, Urga (now known as Ulan Bator) is the capital of Mongolia.

Valkyrie: (Norse mythology) one of the twelve handmaids of Odin (god of war, poetry, knowledge and wisdom) who ride their horses over the field of battle and escort the souls of slain heroes to Valhalla.

whistling post: whistle stop; a small town or community.

White Russian: a Russian who fought against the Bolsheviks (Russian Communist Party) in the Russian Revolution, and fought against the Red Army during the Russian Civil War from 1918 to 1921.

L. Ron Hubbard
in the Golden Age
of Pulp Fiction

*In writing an adventure story
a writer has to know that he is adventuring
for a lot of people who cannot.
The writer has to take them here and there
about the globe and show them
excitement and love and realism.
As long as that writer is living the part of an
adventurer when he is hammering
the keys, he is succeeding with his story.*

*Adventuring is a state of mind.
If you adventure through life, you have a
good chance to be a success on paper.*

*Adventure doesn't mean globe-trotting,
exactly, and it doesn't mean great deeds.
Adventuring is like art.
You have to live it to make it real.*

— *L. RON HUBBARD*

L. Ron Hubbard
and American
Pulp Fiction

Born March 13, 1911, L. Ron Hubbard lived a life at least as expansive as the stories with which he enthralled a hundred million readers through a fifty-year career.

Originally hailing from Tilden, Nebraska, he spent his formative years in a classically rugged Montana, replete with the cowpunchers, lawmen and desperadoes who would later people his Wild West adventures. And lest anyone imagine those adventures were drawn from vicarious experience, he was not only breaking broncs at a tender age, he was also among the few whites ever admitted into Blackfoot society as a bona fide blood brother. While if only to round out an otherwise rough and tumble youth, his mother was that rarity of her time—a thoroughly educated woman—who introduced her son to the classics of Occidental literature even before his seventh birthday.

But as any dedicated L. Ron Hubbard reader will attest, his world extended far beyond Montana. In point of fact, and as the son of a United States naval officer, by the age of eighteen he had traveled over a quarter of a million miles. Included therein were three Pacific crossings to a then still mysterious Asia, where he ran with the likes of Her British Majesty's agent-in-place

L. Ron Hubbard, left, at Congressional Airport, Washington, DC, 1931, with members of George Washington University flying club.

for North China, and the last in the line of Royal Magicians from the court of Kublai Khan. For the record, L. Ron Hubbard was also among the first Westerners to gain admittance to forbidden Tibetan monasteries below Manchuria, and his photographs of China's Great Wall long graced American geography texts.

Upon his return to the United States and a hasty completion of his interrupted high school education, the young Ron Hubbard entered George Washington University. There, as fans of his aerial adventures may have heard, he earned his wings as a pioneering barnstormer at the dawn of American aviation. He also earned a place in free-flight record books for the longest sustained flight above Chicago. Moreover, as a roving reporter for *Sportsman Pilot* (featuring his first professionally penned articles), he further helped inspire a generation of pilots who would take America to world airpower.

Immediately beyond his sophomore year, Ron embarked on the first of his famed ethnological expeditions, initially to then untrammeled Caribbean shores (descriptions of which would later fill a whole series of West Indies mystery-thrillers). That the Puerto Rican interior would also figure into the future of Ron Hubbard stories was likewise no accident. For in addition to cultural studies of the island, a 1932–33

LRH expedition is rightly remembered as conducting the first complete mineralogical survey of a Puerto Rico under United States jurisdiction.

There was many another adventure along this vein: As a lifetime member of the famed Explorers Club, L. Ron Hubbard charted North Pacific waters with the first shipboard radio direction finder, and so pioneered a long-range navigation system universally employed until the late twentieth century. While not to put too fine an edge on it, he also held a rare Master Mariner's license to pilot any vessel, of any tonnage in any ocean.

Yet lest we stray too far afield, there is an LRH note at this juncture in his saga, and it reads in part:

"I started out writing for the pulps, writing the best I knew, writing for every mag on the stands, slanting as well as I could."

To which one might add: His earliest submissions date from the summer of 1934, and included tales drawn from true-to-life Asian adventures, with characters roughly modeled on British/American intelligence operatives he had known in Shanghai. His early Westerns were similarly peppered with details drawn from personal experience. Although therein lay a first hard lesson from the often cruel world of the pulps. His first Westerns were soundly rejected as lacking the authenticity of a Max Brand yarn

Capt. L. Ron Hubbard in Ketchikan, Alaska, 1940, on his Alaskan Radio Experimental Expedition, the first of three voyages conducted under the Explorers Club flag.

(a particularly frustrating comment given L. Ron Hubbard's Westerns came straight from his Montana homeland, while Max Brand was a mediocre New York poet named Frederick Schiller Faust, who turned out implausible six-shooter tales from the terrace of an Italian villa).

Nevertheless, and needless to say, L. Ron Hubbard persevered and soon earned a reputation as among the most publishable names in pulp fiction, with a ninety percent placement rate of first-draft manuscripts. He was also among the most prolific, averaging between seventy and a hundred thousand words a month. Hence the rumors that L. Ron Hubbard had redesigned a typewriter for faster keyboard action and pounded out manuscripts on a continuous roll of butcher paper to save the precious seconds it took to insert a single sheet of paper into manual typewriters of the day.

That all L. Ron Hubbard stories did not run beneath said byline is yet another aspect of pulp fiction lore. That is, as publishers periodically rejected manuscripts from top-drawer authors if only to avoid paying top dollar, L. Ron Hubbard and company just as frequently replied with submissions under various pseudonyms. In Ron's case, the list

A MAN OF MANY NAMES

Between 1934 and 1950,
L. Ron Hubbard authored more than
fifteen million words of fiction in more
than two hundred classic publications.
To supply his fans and editors with
stories across an array of genres and
pulp titles, he adopted fifteen pseudonyms
in addition to his already renowned
L. Ron Hubbard byline.

Winchester Remington Colt
Lt. Jonathan Daly
Capt. Charles Gordon
Capt. L. Ron Hubbard
Bernard Hubbel
Michael Keith
Rene Lafayette
Legionnaire 148
Legionnaire 14830
Ken Martin
Scott Morgan
Lt. Scott Morgan
Kurt von Rachen
Barry Randolph
Capt. Humbert Reynolds

included: Rene Lafayette, Captain Charles Gordon, Lt. Scott Morgan and the notorious Kurt von Rachen—supposedly on the lam for a murder rap, while hammering out two-fisted prose in Argentina. The point: While L. Ron Hubbard as Ken Martin spun stories of Southeast Asian intrigue, LRH as Barry Randolph authored tales of

L. Ron Hubbard, circa 1930, at the outset of a literary career that would finally span half a century.

romance on the Western range—which, stretching between a dozen genres is how he came to stand among the two hundred elite authors providing close to a million tales through the glory days of American Pulp Fiction.

In evidence of exactly that, by 1936 L. Ron Hubbard was literally leading pulp fiction's elite as president of New York's American Fiction Guild. Members included a veritable pulp hall of fame: Lester "Doc Savage" Dent, Walter "The Shadow" Gibson, and the legendary Dashiell Hammett—to cite but a few.

Also in evidence of just where L. Ron Hubbard stood within his first two years on the American pulp circuit: By the spring of 1937, he was ensconced in Hollywood, adopting a Caribbean thriller for Columbia Pictures, remembered today as *The Secret of Treasure Island.* Comprising fifteen thirty-minute episodes, the L. Ron Hubbard screenplay led to the most profitable matinée serial in Hollywood history. In accord with Hollywood culture, he was thereafter continually called

111

The 1937 Secret of Treasure Island, *a fifteen-episode serial adapted for the screen by L. Ron Hubbard from his novel,* Murder at Pirate Castle.

upon to rewrite/doctor scripts—most famously for long-time friend and fellow adventurer Clark Gable.

In the interim—and herein lies another distinctive chapter of the L. Ron Hubbard story—he continually worked to open Pulp Kingdom gates to up-and-coming authors. Or, for that matter, anyone who wished to write. It was a fairly unconventional stance, as markets were already thin and competition razor sharp. But the fact remains, it was an L. Ron Hubbard hallmark that he vehemently lobbied on behalf of young authors—regularly supplying instructional articles to trade journals, guest-lecturing to short story classes at George Washington University and Harvard, and even founding his own creative writing competition. It was established in 1940, dubbed the Golden Pen, and guaranteed winners both New York representation and publication in *Argosy*.

But it was John W. Campbell Jr.'s *Astounding Science Fiction* that finally proved the most memorable LRH vehicle. While every fan of L. Ron Hubbard's galactic epics undoubtedly knows the story, it nonetheless bears repeating: By late 1938, the pulp publishing magnate of Street & Smith was determined to revamp *Astounding Science Fiction* for broader readership. In particular, senior editorial director F. Orlin Tremaine called for stories with a stronger *human element*. When acting editor John W. Campbell balked, preferring his spaceship-driven tales,

Tremaine enlisted Hubbard. Hubbard, in turn, replied with the genre's first truly *character-driven* works, wherein heroes are pitted not against bug-eyed monsters but the mystery and majesty of deep space itself—and thus was launched the Golden Age of Science Fiction.

The names alone are enough to quicken the pulse of any science fiction aficionado, including LRH friend and protégé, Robert Heinlein, Isaac Asimov, A. E. van Vogt and Ray Bradbury. Moreover, when coupled with LRH stories of fantasy, we further come to what's rightly been described as the foundation of every modern tale of horror: L. Ron Hubbard's immortal *Fear.* It was rightly proclaimed by Stephen King as one of the very few works to genuinely warrant that overworked term "classic"—as in: *"This is a classic tale of creeping, surreal menace and horror. . . . This is one of the really, really good ones."*

L. Ron Hubbard, 1948, among fellow science fiction luminaries at the World Science Fiction Convention in Toronto.

To accommodate the greater body of L. Ron Hubbard fantasies, Street & Smith inaugurated *Unknown*—a classic pulp if there ever was one, and wherein readers were soon thrilling to the likes of *Typewriter in the Sky* and *Slaves of Sleep* of which Frederik Pohl would declare: *"There are bits and pieces from Ron's work that became part of the language in ways that very few other writers managed."*

And, indeed, at J. W. Campbell Jr.'s insistence, Ron was regularly drawing on themes from the Arabian Nights and so introducing readers to a world of genies, jinn, Aladdin and Sinbad—all of which, of course, continue to float through cultural mythology to this day.

At least as influential in terms of post-apocalypse stories was L. Ron Hubbard's 1940 *Final Blackout*. Generally acclaimed as the finest anti-war novel of the decade and among the ten best works of the genre ever authored—here, too, was a tale that would live on in ways few other writers

imagined. Hence, the later Robert Heinlein verdict: "Final Blackout *is as perfect a piece of science fiction as has ever been written."*

Like many another who both lived and wrote American pulp adventure, the war proved a tragic end to Ron's sojourn in the pulps. He served with distinction in four theaters and was highly decorated for commanding corvettes in the North Pacific. He was also grievously wounded in combat, lost many a close friend and colleague and thus resolved to say farewell to pulp fiction and devote himself to what it had supported these many years—namely, his serious research.

Portland, Oregon, 1943; L. Ron Hubbard captain of the US Navy subchaser PC 815.

But in no way was the LRH literary saga at an end, for as he wrote some thirty years later, in 1980:

"Recently there came a period when I had little to do. This was novel in a life so crammed with busy years, and I decided to amuse myself by writing a novel that was pure science fiction."

That work was *Battlefield Earth: A Saga of the Year 3000*. It was an immediate *New York Times* bestseller and, in fact, the first international science fiction blockbuster in decades. It was not, however, L. Ron Hubbard's magnum opus, as that distinction is generally reserved for his next and final work: The 1.2 million word *Mission Earth*.

> **Final Blackout**
> *is as perfect a piece of science fiction as has ever been written.*
>
> —Robert Heinlein

How he managed those 1.2 million words in just over twelve months is yet another piece of the L. Ron Hubbard legend. But the fact remains, he did indeed author a ten-volume *dekalogy* that lives in publishing history for the fact that each and every volume of the series was also a *New York Times* bestseller.

Moreover, as subsequent generations discovered L. Ron Hubbard through republished works and novelizations of his screenplays, the mere fact of his name on a cover signaled an international bestseller. . . . Until, to date, sales of his works exceed hundreds of millions, and he otherwise remains among the most enduring and widely read authors in literary history. Although as a final word on the tales of L. Ron Hubbard, perhaps it's enough to simply reiterate what editors told readers in the glory days of American Pulp Fiction:

He writes the way he does, brothers, because he's been there, seen it and done it!

THE STORIES FROM THE GOLDEN AGE

Your ticket to adventure starts here with the Stories from
the Golden Age collection by master storyteller L. Ron Hubbard.
These gripping tales are set in a kaleidoscope of exotic locales and brim
with fascinating characters, including some of the
most vile villains, dangerous dames and brazen heroes
you'll ever get to meet.

The entire collection of over one hundred and fifty stories is being
released in a series of eighty books and audiobooks.
For an up-to-date listing of available titles,
go to www.goldenagestories.com.

AIR ADVENTURE

Arctic Wings	*Man-Killers of the Air*
The Battling Pilot	*On Blazing Wings*
Boomerang Bomber	*Red Death Over China*
The Crate Killer	*Sabotage in the Sky*
The Dive Bomber	*Sky Birds Dare!*
Forbidden Gold	*The Sky-Crasher*
Hurtling Wings	*Trouble on His Wings*
The Lieutenant Takes the Sky	*Wings Over Ethiopia*

FAR-FLUNG ADVENTURE

The Adventure of "X"   *Hurricane*
All Frontiers Are Jealous   *The Iron Duke*
The Barbarians   *Machine Gun 21,000*
The Black Sultan   *Medals for Mahoney*
Black Towers to Danger   *Price of a Hat*
The Bold Dare All   *Red Sand*
Buckley Plays a Hunch   *The Sky Devil*
The Cossack   *The Small Boss of Nunaloha*
Destiny's Drum   *The Squad That Never Came Back*
Escape for Three   *Starch and Stripes*
Fifty-Fifty O'Brien   *Tomb of the Ten Thousand Dead*
The Headhunters   *Trick Soldier*
Hell's Legionnaire   *While Bugles Blow!*
He Walked to War   *Yukon Madness*
Hostage to Death

SEA ADVENTURE

Cargo of Coffins   *The Phantom Patrol*
The Drowned City   *Sea Fangs*
False Cargo   *Submarine*
Grounded   *Twenty Fathoms Down*
Loot of the Shanung   *Under the Black Ensign*
Mister Tidwell, Gunner

118

TALES FROM THE ORIENT

The Devil—With Wings
The Falcon Killer
Five Mex for a Million
Golden Hell
The Green God
Hurricane's Roar
Inky Odds
Orders Is Orders

Pearl Pirate
The Red Dragon
Spy Killer
Tah
The Trail of the Red Diamonds
Wind-Gone-Mad
Yellow Loot

MYSTERY

The Blow Torch Murder
Brass Keys to Murder
Calling Squad Cars!
The Carnival of Death
The Chee-Chalker
Dead Men Kill
The Death Flyer
Flame City

The Grease Spot
Killer Ape
Killer's Law
The Mad Dog Murder
Mouthpiece
Murder Afloat
The Slickers
They Killed Him Dead

119

FANTASY

Borrowed Glory	*If I Were You*
The Crossroads	*The Last Drop*
Danger in the Dark	*The Room*
The Devil's Rescue	*The Tramp*
He Didn't Like Cats	

SCIENCE FICTION

The Automagic Horse	*A Matter of Matter*
Battle of Wizards	*The Obsolete Weapon*
Battling Bolto	*One Was Stubborn*
The Beast	*The Planet Makers*
Beyond All Weapons	*The Professor Was a Thief*
A Can of Vacuum	*The Slaver*
The Conroy Diary	*Space Can*
The Dangerous Dimension	*Strain*
Final Enemy	*Tough Old Man*
The Great Secret	*240,000 Miles Straight Up*
Greed	*When Shadows Fall*
The Invaders	

WESTERN

The Baron of Coyote River	*Man for Breakfast*
Blood on His Spurs	*The No-Gun Gunhawk*
Boss of the Lazy B	*The No-Gun Man*
Branded Outlaw	*The Ranch That No One Would Buy*
Cattle King for a Day	*Reign of the Gila Monster*
Come and Get It	*Ride 'Em, Cowboy*
Death Waits at Sundown	*Ruin at Rio Piedras*
Devil's Manhunt	*Shadows from Boot Hill*
The Ghost Town Gun-Ghost	*Silent Pards*
Gun Boss of Tumbleweed	*Six-Gun Caballero*
Gunman!	*Stacked Bullets*
Gunman's Tally	*Stranger in Town*
The Gunner from Gehenna	*Tinhorn's Daughter*
Hoss Tamer	*The Toughest Ranger*
Johnny, the Town Tamer	*Under the Diehard Brand*
King of the Gunmen	*Vengeance Is Mine!*
The Magic Quirt	*When Gilhooly Was in Flower*

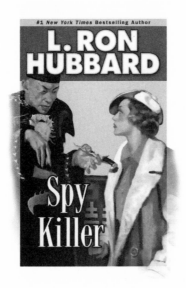

JOIN THE PULP REVIVAL
America in the 1930s and 40s

Pulp fiction was in its heyday and 30 million readers were regularly riveted by the larger-than-life tales of master storyteller L. Ron Hubbard. For this was pulp fiction's golden age, when the writing was raw and every page packed a walloping punch.

That magic can now be yours. An evocative world of nefarious villains, exotic intrigues, courageous heroes and heroines—a world that today's cinema has barely tapped for tales of adventure and swashbucklers.

Enroll today in the Stories from the Golden Age Club and begin receiving your monthly feature edition selected from more than 150 stories in the collection.

You may choose to enjoy them as either a paperback or audiobook for the special membership price of $9.95 each month along with FREE shipping and handling.